NARZEK
FARSEEK WARRIOR SERIES BOOK 2

Clarissa Lake

NARZEK /Clarissa Lake – 2nd ed.
IBSN: 9798527531671

Charissa Lake — 2nd ed.

Please keep in touch:
http://clarissalake.authors.zone/

Visit my website and sign up for my newsletter.

Everyone who signs up will get a free book.

Clarissa Lake's other works:

Narovian Mates Series
Dream Alien
Alien Alliances
Her Alien Captain
Her Alien Trader

Farseek Mercenary Series
Commander's Mate
Lieutenant's Mate
Sahvin's Mate
Argen's Mate
Faigon's Mate

Farseek Warrior Series
Kragyn

Wicked Ways

Interstellar Matchmaking
Korjh's Bride
Rader's Bride
Joven's Bride

Cyborg Awakenings
with Christine Myers
Jolt Somber
Talia's Cyborg
Axel Rex
Dagger Jack

Cyborg Rangers

Blaze

Szeqart Prison Planet Series
Soliv Four
Coraz

ABOUT THE AUTHOR

Clarissa Lake grew up watching Star Trek and reading Marvel Comics. She attended science fiction and fantasy conventions where she met many well-known science fiction authors and attended their readings and discussion panels. They included SciFi greats Anne McCaffery, CJ Cherry, George RR Martin, Ben Bova, Timothy Zahn, Frederik Pohl, Orson Scot Card.

After years of fruitless efforts to get her books published traditionally, she discovered Kindle Direct Publishing and became an Indie author-publisher.

While she loves science fiction, she always thought there should be more romance, so she started writing it hot and steamy.

Contents

Contents

Chapter One

Cayla Fox had been digging weeds for hours under the hot sun using a long-handled hoe with a pointed blade. She paused to take out a rag from her pocket to wipe the sweat from her brow before it started to drip into her eyes. The men and women working the other rows of the crop did the same periodically.

Cayla couldn't fathom that a civilization with interstellar space ships would use slaves to work their fields. Until she was abducted by aliens from Earth over a year ago, she never believed in aliens or that they actually came to Earth and kidnapped people. Yet here she was on an alien world called Berrapo, a slave working in a field under the hot midday sun.

Even though she could probably escape if she planned it out, there was nowhere to go. The slave masters' drones would find her, and the masters would punish her with the pain stick. It was sort of like a cattle prod, but many times more painful. She had learned that lesson the hard way.

She'd had three days of freedom in the nearby forest before they found her. Those three days, she'd had very little food because she didn't know what was edible and what was not on this strange planet. Her military survival training was of little use to her on Berrapo.

At least, here she got to spend time outdoors. On the slave ship, she'd spent the whole time in a dingy, smelly holding cell with eighty other women of various origins and species. The highlight of her days there was when the keeper brought the slop, they called food. It was a bland stew with many vegetables and mystery meat. It was edible though the portions were small.

Hardly a day went by that Cayla didn't wonder what happened to her friend Luanne Field, abducted. The two of them were soldiers, driving through the desert to their next assignment when their vehicle sputtered and died. They called for help, but they were accosted by aliens who looked human. The aliens stunned them with a small weapon.

When they next awoke, they were strapped to bunks inside a spaceship. After they landed on Berrapo, they were separated. Luanne was sent to work in a factory in the city. It wasn't much of a life for either of them.

They'd had dreams for the future after the army to find a nice guy and settle down to have families. That was not likely on Berrapo, where they worked twelve-hour days with one day off in ten. There was no time for socializing because they were too tired to do much more than eat their evening meal and go to bed at the end of their days.

Determination to find a way out kept the threat of hopelessness at bay for Cayla. She would plan better the next time she tried to escape. If she could just get to the spaceport where they came in, maybe she could stow away on a ship. But it was at least an hour away by transport. It could take weeks to walk it. What she didn't know is that all of the slaves were microchipped with trackers. They would be able to find her anywhere on the planet.

Farseek

"Thanks for flying me here," Lieutenant Commander Narzek Pardantu to his warrior friend Kragyn Vermaktu. "The new house is more beautiful than the old one. But my family may never get the chance to live there. I don't know whether they are dead or alive."

"I am glad we only ever saw the damage

in the vids. That was bad enough. I was here when the Sargan's came. One of the blasts knocked me out, and I regained consciousness strapped to a bunk on a slave ship. That's probably what happened to your parents and siblings," said Kragyn.

"That's what I hope; that's why I'm going back out with Dreadnaught Ten."

"You were lucky a lead spot for a ground team opened up," said Kragyn.

"That's because there were more officers like you that found their families alive and well. After fearing them dead for months, they want to spend their time with them."

"I had decided to retire when my contract was up before the Sargan attack. Finding Reanne was the only good thing that came of the whole ordeal." Kragyn said, shaking his head.

Narzek didn't miss the shadow of painful memories that flickered in his eyes. "If I knew one way or another about my family, I would be staying too. Finding them is a longshot. I have to go out there and try."

"As would I. I hope you find them."

"Thanks. We should go back to the starport, so I don't miss my shuttle." Narzek took out his com-tablet and snapped a picture of the new house that replaced the one bombed to rubble in the Sargan attack on

Farseek. "In case I do find them, I can show them they have a home to come back to."

Kragyn nodded, and they started walking back to his personal flyer. It could be called a hybrid shifter. It had wheels so it could be driven on land, or it could hover a couple feet above the ground, and it had retractable wings to fly like a plane. The flyer could stop midair and land vertically. That was the most common use of the flyers because there were few roads between settlements on Farseek.

"I almost wish I could go back out there to help you find your family and more of our people," Kragyn said after they lifted off.

"I appreciate that, but I would be staying if I were in your boots. Besides, Farseek needs experienced warriors right here to defend our world and train new warriors. Your mate and your family need you here."

"And that is why I'm not coming with you."

A few minutes later, they landed at the flyer lot at the newly rebuilt Farseek Spaceport. Both men climbed out, and Kragyn came around to embrace his friend, knowing it could be the last time they ever saw each other.

"Farewell, my friend," said Kragyn, "I will ask the Maker to guide your journey to success."

"Thank you. I'll see you when I get back," Narzek asserted. Even as he said it, somewhere in the back of his mind, he knew it could be a one-way journey.

Narzek turned and pulled his duffle from the cargo compartment and slung the strap over his shoulder. He gave Kragyn a final nod in salute, then strode to the terminal's entrance without looking back.

The new spaceport was built on basically the same layout as the old one, but with some aesthetic improvement. There were only twenty shuttle pads since most of the ships coming to Farseek were freighters too large to land.

Before the Sargan attack, Farseek was a major food crop supplier for the Transtellar Consortium of Worlds. Massive freighters came to transport those crops, distribute them among the other worlds, and bring tech and other goods needed on Farseek. Only, that would not happen again anytime soon.

The population was decimated in the attack and abduction of the survivors. So far, the Farseek Brigade had only brought back around twenty thousand people. Some of those were not Farseekan but were asylum seekers who had also been enslaved by the Sargus Empire.

Thousands had died in the bombings, but they didn't account for a million missing people. Some rescued slaves were abducted from planets in the United Galactic Alliance of Worlds, located in the sector opposite the Consortium. They formed an alliance to bring down the Sargan Empire and recover the people abducted from their worlds. It was a slow process even with military from both federations going from world to world.

The Farseek Warrior Brigade retrieved data from a Pican slave ship that listed worlds where they had delivered people abducted from Farseek. During their time as self-declared mercenaries, the Farseek Warriors had just scratched the surface.

This is why the brigade split their ten-dreadnaught defense force between defending their star system and retrieving their stolen people. Thousands of Farseekans were enslaved throughout a remote string of star systems on the edge of Sargan space.

Although news of the removal of the Sargan Emperor had reached most of the Empire, many worlds still had not freed their slaves nor reported their origins. Each federation in the Alliance could spare only so many military ships for the job. The Farseekans were not content to just go back to their world and wait for others to do the job.

For them, it was personal. Narzek was only one of many that transferred from Farseek star system defense to the slave retrieval force. Many had families still unaccounted for. So, five Farseek Brigade Dreadnaughts took flight back to the Sargus sectors to look for their loved ones and end slavery on the planets where they found them.

Chapter Two

Narzek boarded the shuttle to Dreadnaught Ten, nodding to fellow warriors as he ambled up the center aisle to the next empty seat. The ten-rotation layover on Farseek made him and the others anxious to get back to the mission they had begun over a year ago. His stay on his homeworld was bittersweet. They had made it back to Farseek without their loved ones.

It wasn't hopeless because they had records from the slave ships and the distribution centers that many of their missing family members were taken alive. Even though the Consortium and the Alliance took out Emperor Arbentine Sargus and his whole regime, the worlds under that regime didn't automatically adhere to the declaration that outlawed slavery throughout the empire.

The law would have to be enforced, but they didn't have enough enforcers to administer the edict on every world in the former empire. Both the Consortium and the Alliance encompassed hundreds of planets, and neither had ever eradicated humanoid and sentient beings trafficking by slavers.

In ten short minutes, the shuttle eased into the landing bay on Dread Ten. The forces on each dreadnaught were divided into teams of ground fighters and starship operations. The dreadnaughts were as heavily armed as most battlecruisers but more compacted, requiring smaller crews. Each of the dreadnaughts carried 150—200 personnel. Only the best of the best warriors made it into the Farseek Brigade. Their small force could do things that larger star fleets would not attempt. Besides, they had some of the best tech available.

Narzek was the new team leader for a team of nine warriors who had transferred in as he had. They had thirty rotations to train and function as a team before reaching the first star systems where their people were sent. All five dreadnaughts were spaced out on the same course, so they didn't all get to a star system simultaneously.

The designated scout would arrive first for reconnaissance. By the time the others came, they would know where the most prominent groups of Farseekans were held. On the more densely populated worlds like Berrapo, they needed all the ground teams from all the dreads on the ground to search for their people and any other people enslaved by

Sargans.

Narzek was glad to have the lead in time to prepare his team for that mission. They were all good men and women, seasoned warriors; they just needed time to learn their functions in the unit. It was almost dull how everyone performed as they should, but they kept training to fill the time until they went ground-side to start their rescue operation.

The *Kurellis*, a huge passenger ship they stole from the Sargans at Tegliar Station, came with them to carry the rescues back to Farseek or where ever they might wish to go along the way. Its maximum capacity was ten thousand and maybe a few hundred more if they doubled up.

The nights alone in his quarters were the hardest for Narzek. That's when his imagination haunted him of all the horrible things that could have happened to his mother, brother, and sisters. They had all heard the horror stories.

The worst part was that Farseek Brigade was off fighting in the Sargus Empire when Sargans attacked Farseek. The plan made and executed by Evzen Guryan, Governor of Halor and member of the Consortium High Council was born of pure greed. He was caught and punished for his treachery and was of little comfort to those whose families were missing over two years.

Guryon had been stripped of his vast holdings and all of his political power. He had once lived in a palatial mansion; he now occupied a tiny prison cell, sentenced to life in prison. That wasn't enough as far as Narzek and many other warriors were concerned. Even if it were allowed by law, torturing him every day for the rest of his life would not be enough for the thousands killed and a million people unaccounted for.

Narzek would go to the gym and perform a meditative exercise similar to tai chi when he couldn't sleep. During one such session, it came to him that his negative feelings about Evzen Guryon and his missing family were detrimental to him, not the people responsible for his anguish. They were stealing his energy and focusing his mind on those negative feelings. That negativity was sapping his fervor for the task ahead.

Whether he found his family or not, he was doing what he could to find them. If he never located them, he still had memories of spending a happy childhood with them until he went to warrior training at sixteen. Barring the odds, he could possibly find them. He could not change the past; there was no use dwelling on it.

Going back would put Narzek and half of the Farseek Brigade back in the warzone. The military forces still loyal to the Emperor refused to surrender and declared war on the Consortium and the Alliance. He might not find any of his lost family, and he could die trying.

Cayla's body ached at the end of every day when she finally climbed into her bunk. What she wouldn't give for a shower and a clean nightgown to wear to bed. She might as well wish for a miracle to get her off this miserable planet so she could go home. But if she ever found her way back to Earth, she could face charges for desertion and AWOL. She almost laughed as she wondered if being abducted by alien slavers off the face of the Earth would get them to drop the charges.

They slept on bare mattresses in their clothes as that was all they had to wear. Cayla might have worn her underwear only to bed, except it had worn out months ago. They were each given one blanket that most of them used for pillows because it was always hot in the barracks.

She didn't have trouble sleeping anymore. Her exhausting workload left her too tired to lament over the past or worry about the future. She fell asleep within minutes of closing her eyes, and this night was no different.

It seemed like minutes after she had fallen asleep that a ruckus teased her awareness at the edge of a dream. Suddenly, the bright overhead lights came on to moans and groans of the women who had been sleeping. How could it be morning already? Then came the voice of explanation.

"Ladies, please listen. I am Lieutenant Commander Narzek Pardantu of the Farseek Brigade," he said from the front of the room. He paused as a few women shouted their approval. "Slavery has been abolished in the Sargan Empire, and we have come to free you and take you home to Farseek. Please dress and gather any belongings, and we will take you to the shuttle up to the passenger ship."

"Farseek?" Cayla muttered. She pulled on her boots and jumped down from her bunk, walking over to the man who had spoken. He was quite a bit taller than her, 5'7" and clad in some kind of body armor with his headgear retracted to reveal a handsome face and a bit of bristly platinum hair.

"Commander Pardantu, I'm not from Farseek. I'm from Earth. I'd kind of like to go home," Cayla told him.

He sniffed and looked at her with a slight frown. She almost expected a curt retort. It probably sounded ungrateful to the man who had just announced he was freeing them from slavery.

The commander blinked a couple times and shook his head, then said just one word, "*solmatu.*"

"I'm sorry, what?" It was a word that didn't translate, like many other words with the inferior translator chip the slavers injected into her.

"Maker, I'm not ready for this." But his expression softened as he looked down at her. "It will take some explaining, but we have thousands of people to get off this planet. Will you tell me your name?"

"Cayla Fox. Before I was a slave, I was a soldier back on Earth. I was in a warzone when those slavers stole my friend and me."

"That should make things a little easier. I need you to come to our ship, the Farseek Dreadnaught Ten. We've got another farm to evacuate, then I will be back to explain," he said cryptically. Then he said, "open comm. Lieutenant Commander Pardantu to Commander Lagatu."

Cayla could only hear the LC's end of the conversation, but it didn't shed any light on the situation.

"I am declaring *solmatu,* Cayla Fox of Earth. I'm sending her to Dread Ten." He paused. "Thank you, sir. No, sir. We've got at least a thousand people to move from our assigned locations. That comes first." He paused to listen again. "Affirmative, sir. Pardantu out."

"I won't even ask," said Cayla. "Tell me how I can help."

"Are there more than four slave barracks, and do the guards have weapons?"

"Only four, here. The slave masters have pain sticks but no other weapons. When they touch you with them, it seems like every pain receptor in your body is on fire," said Cayla. "We've all felt it a time or two. They are not allowed to damage us. But they do other things...."

"To you?" he demanded.

"No." Cayla shook her head.

"Good, you can best help us by making sure we have everyone who wants to leave."

"What are the chances I can get back to Earth someday?"

"It's possible, but right now, we need to get these people moving."

"Of course," Cayla said, but she found herself staring at him. There was something about him that attracted her and made her feel reluctant to leave his presence. But he was right; whatever this unspoken awareness between them was, it needed to wait.

Chapter Three

Cayla helped herd the rest of the women from the slave barracks to the waiting shuttles. For the first time in almost ever, most of the women were smiling. Their people had come for them, just like they always told her they would. Cayla was happy for them and herself, too. Even though the chance of getting back to Earth was uncertain, at least she would no longer be a slave.

She had a feeling about the LC and what he wasn't telling her. He was one of the hottest guys she'd ever met. Whatever was going on, one of her first thoughts on meeting him was that she might like getting to know him better. He must be thinking along those lines. Why else was he sending her to his warship instead of the passenger ship where everyone else went?

The shuttle barely touched down in the landing bay of the dreadnaught before she was shown the door where she was met by a young man in a military uniform.

"I'm Tagnel. I'll be your guide for now. We will stop at the storeroom to get you fresh clothes, then I will take you to your quarters where you can shower and get some rest since they woke you in the middle of your night."

"Can you tell me why I was brought here instead of the passenger ship?" she asked.

"It's not for me to say, *se'atu*. These are my orders," Tagnel said. "I'm sure the Lieutenant Commander has his reasons. No one shared them with me."

"But you have some idea."

"I wouldn't speculate."

Cayla chuckled. "They told you to keep your mouth shut."

"Yes, *se'atu*." He grinned faintly.

"All right, then. Lead on Tagnel."

He nodded and led her through the cargo bay to the storeroom. "*Se'atu*, you will stand on that circle, the scanner in the ceiling will determine your size, and a bot will bring you clothes in that size.

Cayla did as she was asked, "What is '*se'atu*'? It doesn't translate."

"It is a Uatu word used to address a young unmated female. The main Consortium language doesn't include translations for most Uatu root words. Farseek was originally settled by Uatu people from a distant world called Uat. We grow up learning the ancient language as well as Consortium preferred."

"So, what happened to end slavery in the Sargan Empire?" Cayla wondered.

"The Consortium and the United Galactic Alliance of Worlds became allies and took out the Emperor. They are now in the process of conquering his fleet. They are too busy now to return the people enslaved by the Sargans to their homeworlds, so we are searching for them ourselves."

"Where's the Alliance from?"

"They are on the far side of the Sargan Sectors.

"Are they anywhere near Earth?"

"I-I'm not sure."

Cayla could see that he was hedging again. She didn't get a chance to ask him anymore because the droid brought her clothing packed into a small duffle. Tagnel took the duffle from the droid to carry it for her and started heading down the narrow corridor.

"This way," was all he said. Near the end, he stopped in front of a lift, and the door slid open. He stepped inside, and Cayla followed.

It didn't look much like the ships on Star Trek. It was much more utilitarian, and space seemed to be at a premium. The young warrior showed her to a cabin that was about ten feet square with a built-in bed with a small closet at one end and storage drawers underneath. There was a wider door at the other end of the bed.

Tagnel set the duffle on the bed, then went to the larger door and gave a command, and it opened. "This is your sanitary closet. Here are the retractable toilet and waterless hand cleaning dispenser. With the toilet retracted, this becomes your shower. Water is at a premium here, and every drop is purified and recycled. The water comes in cycles. A short burst wets you, then you apply the cleaning solution to your hair and body. Then you call for a rinse. The whole process takes less than three mini-spans."

"What about towels?"

"It dries you with warm air," he said. "Then you may want to get some rest. It could be several spans before the LC returns." He went on to tell her the commands for the room functions.

"Thank you, Tagnel."

The young man snapped to attention and dipped his head in what Cayla guessed was a salute. "*Se'atu.*"

He then did an about-face and retreated out of the cabin.

When he was gone, Cayla did a slow turn around the cabin. Against the wall beside the door was a small square table with rounded edges with two built-in seats facing each other and a darkened screen on the wall. The cabin was nothing fancy, but it was better than sleeping in a barracks in a bunk bed with over 80 other women.

She went to the duffle on the bed to look at the clothing Tagnel gave her. There was a brand-new pair of boots on top of three pairs of black cargo-type pants and three tops, all in black. Underneath were two pairs of gray boxer-type shorts and matching tank tops. Cayla stowed the clothing in the drawers and kept out a tank set to wear to bed after she showered.

She gave the privacy command and sat on the edge of the bed to untie and remove her military boots. She stripped off the ragged desert, camo fatigues and dropped them on the floor. She walked into the shower closet nude and went through the cycle just as Tagnel had explained.

It felt delightful to be clean. Though she was a little anxious to find out what was going on, she was exhausted. Cayla put on the soft, comfortable tank set and picked up her boots and fatigues from the floor, and stowed them in the empty closet along with the duffle. She would have discarded them, but she didn't know where to do that.

Finally, she turned back the thin sheet on

the bed and lowered herself onto it, delighted to find a real pillow at the head. She had so many questions circling in her mind about what was happening and whether they would discover Luanne at one of the factories if she were still alive.

She was just too tired to speculate. Instead, she closed her eyes and cleared her mind, taking slow, deep breaths. Inhale, exhale, inhale, exhale, relaxing her muscles as she did, and finally, she slept.

Several spans later, Narzek stopped in the corridor at the door of Cayla's cabin. It was still set to 'privacy.' He rested his hand on the door and sighed. Although he had the authority to override it, he didn't. He'd been working twenty spans straight, and he was so tired he was almost asleep on his feet.

He would come back later after they had both rested, and he could think a little straighter. He stood there for some micro-spans convincing himself to set his body in motion to go to his cabin a few doors down.

Once inside, he toed his boots to retract from his feet and fell into his bunk fully clothed and murmured one word. *"Solmatu."*

Chapter Four

Cayla had wakened refreshed, though with no idea how long she had slept. She took out a set of the clothing she'd been given and started to pull on the pants over the boxer shorts when she realized there was a liner within them. It was the same for the matching shirt, as it had built-in breast support.

She had just pulled the shirt on when she heard a kind of chirping noise. Guessing it might be the door alert, she gave the command to open it. She was still in her bare feet but otherwise fully clothed.

Cayla was not surprised to see LC Pardantu standing there with a tray of drinks and two covered dishes.

"May I enter?" he asked.

Cayla nodded, and he stepped inside. She opened her mouth to speak, but nothing came out as her eyes met his. His gaze was intense, and his pale blue eyes were a shade she had rarely seen. This time she knew she hadn't imagined the attraction that seemed to reverberate between them.

"I haven't eaten since last rotation, so I thought you might be hungry as well," he said, breaking the silence.

"Sure, now that you mention it, I am hungry, thank you."

That was all the invitation Narzek needed to carry the tray over to the small table. He set the tray down and took the seat against the wall. Cayla padded across the floor, still barefoot, and took the other chair.

"I don't know what you normally eat, so I picked a few of the things we normally have at first meal," he said, setting a covered plate in front of her, a steamy mug of liquid. "The mug is slightly sweetened tea. It contains a mild stimulant, which is mainly why we drink it."

Narzek uncovered her plate and then his own and set them on the tray off to the side.

Cayla couldn't identify anything on the plate, but it smelled good—a small bowl of steamy mush that looked a bit like oatmeal, possibly a meat patty, and some assorted pieces of fruit. "I'm sure it's okay. It looks and smells better than the stuff they fed us at the farm.

She picked up a utensil that was a spoon with three short tines and the serrated knife on her plate and cut a piece of the meat patty. Popping it into her mouth, she chewed it, concentrating on the flavor. It tasted a bit like lamb with some mild spices that enhanced the flavor.

"Not bad," she said. "But I'm not that fussy. I'm used to army chow." She paused to take another bite. "So, Lieutenant Commander Pardantu, are you going to tell me why I'm here on this warship instead of the passenger transport with the others."

His gaze was openly admiring, yet he seemed to hesitate with the answer to her question. "Because you are *solmatu*---my *solmatu*," he said finally. "Please call me Narzek."

"Okay, Narzek. That must be one of those ancient Uatu words that don't translate with my inferior translator."

"Is it so hard to figure out? Can you tell me that you don't feel the powerful attraction between us?"

Did she feel it? Oh, yeah! Her girly parts came to life for the first time in—too long. She was almost afraid to get too close because they might rub sparks off each other.

"Are we even the same species? You look human enough, but I haven't seen that skin color variation before." His skin was a light lavender blue.

"I am human. Humans are sprinkled all over this galaxy, maybe others. The Uatu people have a kind of sixth sense that allows them to recognize their soul mates. That is *solmatu*. You are my, *solmatu*," he explained. "I knew as soon as I caught your scent. I wanted to stop everything and take you somewhere to get to know each other, but I couldn't. So, I had you brought here until I finished my assignment. If I let you go with the others to the passenger ship, it could be a sun span before I might see you again."

Cayla could only guess, but in that context, he probably meant about a year. "I see. What is customary when you recognize your soul mate?"

"I declare *solmatu* to my commander, which gives me the right to have you onboard our ship so I can court you," he said, never taking his eyes from her face. "To spend time with you so you can decide if you wish to become my mate for life."

"Oh." Cayla frowned. She didn't know what she expected, but that wasn't it. Initially, she thought maybe he just wanted to get laid and maybe have a fling for a few weeks or whatever time standard they used. "Wow."

"You don't have to decide whether to become my life mate now. We have a few weeks before we get to the next star system on our route, time for us to become better acquainted before you decide."

"There is no way I can get back to Earth, is there?"

"It could be arranged, but it would take some time," he admitted reluctantly. "We would have to rendezvous with an Alliance ship, then they would arrange transport to Earth." He looked even more disheartened as he said the last.

Cayla reached across the table and put her hand over his. "It's nothing against you, LC. My parents probably think I am dead. I was in a war zone when they kidnapped me. It's not like I can call them up and let them know I'm okay."

"We can arrange to get word back to them. Earth is now a member of the Alliance, and they can relay a vid message to them. They've done it for other Earthers. Or are you determined to go there?"

Narzek turned his hand so he could hold hers. Now that she was touching him, she began to feel that unspoken connection between them. There was kindness in his eyes and longing. This man didn't just want to get laid. He wanted to love and be loved.

Whether or not he really was her soul mate, Cayla was intensely attracted to him. Getting word to her parents was really the most important thing. If she went back, she'd probably spend a couple weeks with them and go back to the army and finish her tour.

Watching her face, he brought her hand up to his lips and kissed it. She sucked in her breath audibly as she felt that kiss all the way to her core. Suddenly, the thought of going back to Earth and never seeing Narzek again was not all that appealing.

Narzek stood up and pulled her into his arms. Cayla instinctively looked up at him, parting her lips to accept his kiss as he lowered his mouth to hers. At first, it was a gentle caress of lips, and then his tongue slipped into her mouth as he deepened the kiss. He pressed her body tightly to his so her breasts were squeezed against his firm chest.

Her heart was racing, and her core was throbbing as she felt his erection against her belly. The kiss went on and on until they were both trembling with desire, and Cayla could not think of one reason why not to just fuck him. She had never wanted a man the way she wanted him.

She was just about to throw caution to the wind when Narzek pulled back.

"I'm not trying to rush you into bed; I just wanted you to understand what is between us, what we could have together," he said a little tightly.

"Yeah, that was pretty hot," Cayla said as

her cheeks grew warm. "Maybe we should sit back down and finish our breakfast."

"Break fast?"

"First meal of the day." She sat back down and took up the fork-spoon thing to get a bite of warm mush from her bowl. It tasted similar to oatmeal but slightly nuttier.

Eating was good, and it would keep their bodies from getting ahead of their intellects. Narzek gave her a wry grin and took his seat as well.

"When we finish eating, would you like me to show you around the ship?" he asked.

"Sure," she said, thinking that was probably a safe move. "I've been on a couple ships since I was abducted, but all I saw of them was the dingy room they crammed us into."

"Damn slavers. The Consortium has been at war with the Sargan's for solar spans. Then we made a peace agreement with them. They agreed to stop abducting our people for slavery," Narzek explained. "But it was a lie. While we were fighting for the Consortium, the Sargans bombed our world and stole our people."

"That's terrible. I met a lot of females from Farseek on the ship that brought us to Berrapo. I half expected I would end up as a sex slave in a brothel when I was kidnapped.

Instead, they brought us to this farm labor camp."

"After our world was attacked, the Consortium released us from our contract to help defend our worlds. Nearly every warrior lost members of their family to the Sargans. Some were killed, and others were stolen to become slave labor for the Empire."

"Your family is missing, too," Cayla said.

"Yes." He nodded grimly. "All except my father. He's an officer on Dread Eight. The Consortium had our family home rebuilt, but without our family, it's not really home anymore."

"I am so sorry."

"It's not your fault. Why should you be sorry?"

"In our culture, that's what we say to someone who has such a loss. When I say I am sorry, it is understood that I am sorry that you suffered the loss of your family."

"Ah, then the proper response would be 'thank you'?"

Cayla nodded and smiled at him.

Chapter Five

"Do you think some of them might have been rescued from the other work sites?"

"The liaison from the passenger ship was still adding people to our database. The AI will notify us if any of our family members are located," he said.

"Could you find out if Luanne Field was taken to the passenger ship?"

He nodded and took out a small communication tablet the reminded Cayla of a smartphone. "AI Dreadnaught Ten, this is Pardantu. Please add Luanne Field to my list of persons I am seeking."

Then he stood. "Shall we go?"

"I just need to get these new boots on, but they won't open, and they didn't give me any socks."

"Socks?"

"Foot covering to wear under your boots."

"These are smart boots with a self-cleaning liner."

Cayla walked over to the bed and picked them up from the floor. Narzek followed, and she handed him one of the boots. He turned it to heel and pointed to a circular depression in the center, then pushed it. The boot opened into three flaps.

Narzek hunkered down, setting the boot on the floor. "Put your foot there." He pointed to the insole. With her foot in place, he pushed the button again, and the flaps closed over her foot snugly but not too tight. "Now, you try it." He stood beside her, watching.

Cayla held the boot in her hand and pressed the button. Setting it on the floor, she stepped into it and squatted down to press the button again. It wrapped around her foot, just like the other boot.

"They feel pretty good, and they look smart, too," she said and winked at him at the pun. They were shiny black to match the black uniforms.

Narzek gave her a faint smile. "While I show you around, we can stop at the medical bay, and you can get a state-of-the-art language chip that will allow you to speak and read Consortium within a day or two."

"Will it hurt?"

"Not a bit." He smiled. "Let's go before I have to kiss you again."

Cayla nodded. She knew she would like that way too much. As they left her cabin, Narzek guided her resting his hand lightly on the small of her back as they walked the hallway. On their way to the lift, he pointed out his cabin, which was one door down the corridor from hers.

There were three levels of crew quarters with the mess and conference room on the second level. The gym and the training rooms were adjacent to the armory and the landing bay on the first level. The engineering level was under level one, housing the weapons arrays and the engines. Level four held the bridge and officer suites.

The fourth level was heavily shielded beneath the fifth level, maintaining access to the weapons arrays on the top deck. Although the Farseek dreadnaughts were small by warship standards, the ship seemed huge to Cayla.

"For a ground fighter, you know an awful lot about the ship," Cayla said.

"We all cross-train in case we have to take over operating the ship. It's never happened, but it could. Every member of the Farseek Brigade had combat training as well."

"If I stay here with you, what will I do? My combat training didn't prepare me for anything like this."

"That's partly up to you. As my *solmatu*, you are not required to serve," he said.

Cayla just gave him a look that required no translation.

"However, once your language upload takes effect, you can test to see what positions you have an aptitude for in the brigade."

"That makes sense," she said. "Obviously, I have a lot to learn. I would have been a transport driver in a warzone back on Earth. No big trucks here."

"I'm guessing that is a land vehicle," Narzek said.

"Yes."

"Now that I showed you the mess, there isn't much left to see on the other residential levels. I will take you up to see the bridge. Normally, you would be restricted from entering there, but I want to show you our holographic star map."

"That sounds interesting."

"When we first rescued abductees from Earth, we didn't know where that world was located. After we rescued two people from the Alliance, one was able to contact them, and they gave us the information we needed."

"But it's far. I know it took a long time for that slave ship to get us to Berrapo. Three or four months, at least."

"Yes, and it is still too dangerous for routine transports to cross Sargan space to get there. Even though we took down the Emperor, their Starfleet has not surrendered.

They've taken over running it, engaging both Consortium and Alliance battleships at every opportunity," he explained as they strolled toward the lift.

"And we're right in the middle of it?"

"Yes. The Farseek Brigade was officially exempt from continuing the war against the Sargus Empire, but they won't differentiate our activities if they catch us. We're stealing their slaves."

"So, I've traded one warzone for another."

Narzek nodded grimly. "I am torn about that, even though we are just getting acquainted. I want to keep you safe, but I want you to be here." He needed her to be there with him. Once he had held her and kissed her, he knew she was his.

"Don't be." Cayla turned toward him and touched his arm as the lift door closed. "I owe your people for getting me out of slavery, and I know there is something potent between us."

Narzek took her over to the enormous star map displayed from floor to ceiling behind the crew workstations when they reached the bridge. Cayla was awed by it even though she couldn't read the labels on the stars.

"Cayla Fox, meet Zajha Damektu, our Chief Navigator."

Zajha dipped her head in salute, and Cayla

returned the gesture.

"I brought Cayla here to show her where her homeworld, Earth, is compared to where we are."

"It is very far," Zajha said. With a sweep of her hand, she compressed the hologram to include the Sol system. Then she pointed to Earth's star.

Cayla immediately saw how much she had to shrink the display to include Berrapo and Earth in the stars scape. Even then, Sol and Berrapo were at the opposite end on a higher plane of the map. Then Zajha showed the spatial relationship between Berrapo and Farseek. Farseek was half the distance from the Sargan world as Earth.

"Narzek probably told you that we would have to contact the Alliance to arrange a rendezvous with one of their battleships to get you back to Earth," said Zajha.

Cayla nodded.

"Even then, I could be a while before they could arrange for an Alliance transport ship to meet up with the battleship. Personally, I think you're safer with us. We are faster and just as well-armed as their larger battleships."

"I'm not in a hurry to leave. Narzek is doing his best to convince me to stay."

"Yes, I heard that he declared *solmatu.*

Congratulations to you both." Zajha smiled sincerely as she said it. "So many of us have lost some or all of our families; finding our *solmatu* is heartening for morale."

"Not too many secrets on this ship," Narzek said. "It was no different on Dread Four. Thank you for showing us the map. Now I am taking Cayla to medical to get a proper language chip."

As they left the bridge, Narzek rested his hand lightly on the small of her back, giving no other outward signal of their budding relationship. The lift was empty when they walked in. Narzek gave a command and then pulled Cayla into his arms and proceeded to kiss her breathless.

Holding her tightly against him, as he plundered her mouth urgently, one of his hands slid down to her buttocks, pressing her belly tightly against his erection. Cayla hugged him back as her body clamored for more. She raised herself on her toes so that her throbbing clit was pressing against his engorged cock.

Somewhere in the back of her mind, she knew they shouldn't be doing this in the lift, but she didn't have the will to pull back. Only when a chime sounded did Narzek break the kiss reluctantly and release her, smoothing her hair as he commanded the lift to continue to the lowest level. He gave her a rueful smile and a smoldering look as the elevator stopped and the doors opened.

Fortunately, only an autocart was waiting to deliver supplies to the various floors. There was no one there to witness Cayla's slightly disheveled appearance and the bulge in Narzek's trousers.

Chapter Six

"The Uatu people generally do not display affection publicly, but I couldn't help risking it. You are so beautiful and desirable," Narzek said close to her ear.

Cayla sighed. "Well, I wasn't exactly pushing you away." She paused and glanced around. They were alone, not that she was worried. She knew it would only be a matter of time before they gave in to their mutual desire. "This is where we came in, isn't it?"

"Yes. The ship was designed so that sickbay was close to the landing bay to get treatment for warriors injured in battle as quickly as possible. This way," he said, steering her to an open doorway with a sign on the ceiling in their alien script.

The handsome young man who greeted them had reddish skin and orange hair. It might have been a color choice, but it appeared to be entirely natural.

"Hello, Tor'ien. This is Cayla Fox of Earth. She needs a full Consortium language upload," Narzek said.

"So, this is your *solmatu*," Tor'ien smiled cordially. "She is so pale, but she certainly looks human."

"She is human," Narzek said.

"We come in a few different colors on Earth, but not quite so varied as you. My friend Luanne has light brown skin and dark hair," Cayla said. "So, how is your language implant better than the one the slavers put in?"

"Because we write it onto your own DNA. Come inside, and I will explain." He showed them both into a small treatment room that contained a lounge chair, much like one in a dental office. "Have a seat, and I will get the specimen kit."

The medic went to a small cupboard and took out a test tube with a swab inside it. "First, I will swab inside your cheek for some cells, then we will turn them into a language module, then squirt them into your nose."

Cayla opened her mouth as Tor'ien held the swab poised in front of her. He returned the swab to the test tube. "This will take just a few mini-spans."

"That sounds easy enough," Cayla said, with a smile for Narzek. He picked up her hand and held it rubbing the back of it with his thumb.

Moments later, the medic returned with a small plastic syringe. "Just a little squirt up your nose…" he inserted the tip into her left nostril and pushed the plunger. "Now, breathe in, so it goes all the way up into your sinus cavity."

She did.

"Okay, while I have you here, let's get a body scan to make sure you haven't picked up any bugs during your stay with the Sargans," he said. "Everyone we rescued from Berrapo is being scanned. Just stay still, and it will be quick. Begin scan."

He'd barely finished the command when a short beep signaled it was over. Tor'ien glanced at the readout. "Shows some normal variations, but no parasites or disease processes. You may proceed with normal activities."

"Thank you, Doctor," Cayla said.

"Just Medic," Tor'ien said. "You're welcome."

"Where to next?" Cayla asked as she stood.

"Well, I've shown you all I can without clearance, except for the gym and the physical training rooms. Or I could show you my quarters."

"Right. I think I'd like to see the gym." After what happened in the lift, Cayla knew what would happen in his quarters. The level of attraction between them was unlike anything she had ever felt. Yet, it was more than that. She liked him, and from the way he looked at her, he wanted her, too.

"I heard wonderful things about your world because many women in our barracks were from your world. They never stopped believing that your Farseek Brigade would come for them. It was only a matter of when."

"Yes." He nodded with a grim expression. "Most of us lost family and friends in and after that attack."

"I suppose we were lucky to be sent to Berrapo, despite the fact we were slaves. They made us work long hours in the fields, and the food was barely palatable, but we were not severely abused like some of those on the slave ship."

"That's good to know," he said as they began walking.

They hadn't gotten far when Narzek's com-tablet beeped from his pocket. He took it out and read the message on the screen. "Thank the Maker!" he murmured excitedly.

"What?"

"One of my sisters was found at another location on Berrapo. Your friend Luanne as well," he said wondrously.

"Can we call them with your device?" Cayla hesitated to call it a phone because

Narzek had alluded that it was much more. It was capable of producing holographic images of people at both ends of the conversation, so it was almost like they were in the same room talking together.

"Not yet. Communications are tied up, reporting all the Uatu people who we retrieved to their loved ones. They will contact us in a rotation or two."

Narzek sighed, looking relieved and disappointed at the news. Cayla could understand such mixed feelings. She was grateful to be freed from slavery yet disappointed that she might never get back to Earth.

Narzek dropped the com in his pocket then hugged her without warning, lifting her off her feet. She thought for a moment he would kiss her, but he stopped and seemed to shake himself mentally. In the middle of the hallway, close to the gym, anyone could come by at any time.

He set her back on her feet and broke contact as soon as she had her balance. Cayla was a bit stunned by the desire coursing through her body by that brief contact.

Narzek looked up and down the corridor.

"Don't worry. No one saw that," Cayla murmured.

She doubted he was embarrassed as she

saw the raw need in his eyes when she looked up at him. He was an officer, and even though he was off duty, she suspected he could be disciplined had anyone seen them.

"I need you to come with me," he murmured urgently. "I need you."

He looked shaken between the news and the explosion of desire that flared between them whenever they touched. Cayla had some of those same feelings, adding to all the craziness that had become her life. With Narzek, she had found a bond worth pursuing. She nodded and started heading for the lift.

They didn't speak or touch as the doors closed. When they emerged on their level, Cayla let him guide her to the door of his quarters. Once they were inside, Narzek turned to her and cradled her face in his hands.

"If you are not ready for me to claim you as my mate, I wish to share sex with you?"

"What is the difference?"

"Once I eject my seed inside you, we are bonded for life. But I can wear a collector on my cock. It will not affect your pleasure or mine."

"Yes, do that." She wasn't ready to make a commitment. She barely knew Narzek. What she did know was that she wanted him.

"Even then, I don't think I can ever let you go. *Solmatu* only comes once in a lifetime."

"I don't share sex lightly, Narzek. I believe that this *solmatu* is real. I have never wanted a man as much as I want you right now."

Cayla could see the hunger in his eyes as he stared into hers for several seconds before he covered her lips with his in a tender kiss. As his mouth moved against hers, she opened for him; their only contact was their lips and his hands framing her face.

Narzek took her invitation to slide his tongue into her mouth and swirl it around hers. He pulled her against him and lifted her up, so they were chest to chest, and Cayla wrapped her legs around his hips, so her mons was pressed against his erection.

Cayla knew this was happening fast, but she knew she wanted it. Two years of her life had been stolen from her, and she wanted the pleasure she found in Narzek's arms. For those same two years, Cayla was a slave; his life had been in limbo, not knowing if his family was dead or alive.

Even with the good news he just received, his mother's fate was still unknown. They both needed an outlet for the turmoil of their emotions. No matter what happened, Cayla refused to feel guilty for having sex with this man she met a day ago.

Still kissing her, Narzek stopped in front of his bedroom off his small sitting area inside the entryway. He cupped her buttocks in his hands, helping to support her weight, and ground his erection against her crotch. Cayla moaned into his mouth as she felt the pressure against her clit.

There was no going back.

Chapter Seven

Inside Narzek's bedroom, they kissed feverishly while clothes came off, landing in a heap on the floor. He meant to go slow, but his cock was so hard it almost hurt. Ever since he sensed the solmatu pheromones, it became harder to suppress his desire for her. He paused to look at her once he'd divested her of her clothing.

Although she was a little too thin, probably from her months of hard labor and short rations, she was the most beautiful female he had ever seen. Despite his aching need, he paused to cradle her face in his hands, stroking her cheeks with his thumbs. There was tenderness in her eyes, and she gave him a shy smile.

Narzek kissed her forehead, then her mouth lightly at first. As he deepened the kiss, he wrapped his arms around her and pressed her body tight to his.

Cayla raised on her toes, so his cock slid between her legs, and its length rested against her folds. She wound her arms around his neck and arched her back, rubbing her breasts against the wall of his chest. He staked his claim with his tongue inside her mouth, and she stroked it with hers.

They were still kissing as he lowered them onto the bed, not bothering to push back the thin top cover. She was beneath him, cradling his hips between her thighs, her legs bent with her feet flat on the bed. He could feel she was completely wet for him against his cock, so he reached for the panel at the head of the bed. It opened as he touched it, and he took out a single packet, tore it open, and took out the small thin disk the size of a small coin.

Raising himself up, he pressed the disk to the tip of his cock. It immediately expanded to encase the full length of his cock in a micro-thin high-tech lubricated condom.

"I am ready," Cayla whispered, "I need you now."

"And I need you." He held his weight over her on one forearm and used his other hand to guide the head of his cock into her opening. He stared into her eyes as he slid his length into her, and her inner walls stretched to accommodate him.

"Ah, Narzek. Mm."

He groaned his pleasure and lowered his weight against her feeling the tips of her beaded nipples against his chest. She put her arms around him, rubbing her hands up and down his back.

He brought up his hand to cup her cheek as he planted butterfly kisses over her face, murmuring, "*solmatu*" as an endearment. *His solmatu.*

Being in her and on her was a pleasure like nothing he had ever felt before, and he meant to savor every mini-span. Finally, when he had kissed her face all over and nibbled on her neck and earlobes, he started pumping in and out of her slowly, committing to memory every delicious sensation of the first time making love to his soul mate.

It didn't matter whether he claimed her now or later. Cayla was his. He was claiming her with every stroke of his cock as he thrust it into her. As he pumped harder and faster, he kissed her, thrusting his tongue into her mouth as he thrust his cock into her center.

He pounded into her harder and faster, eliciting a little groan from her with each stroke. Yet she met every one eagerly, crooning his name as an endearment and panting as he took her closer to release.

Her muscles tensed as she clung to him, and her short nails stung just a little as they dug into his back. Then she cried his name, and her inner walls contracted around his cock with the first wave of her orgasm. She writhed beneath him, and that was enough to take him over the top as well.

Cayla hugged him as he kissed her, his cock still throbbing inside her as his seed was contained in the condom. Each time his cock pulsed inside her, a new wave of orgasmic contractions massaged his length.

"Somehow, I knew it would be intense between us, and that surely was," she said, kissing him lightly. She smiled up at him, caressing his face and running her fingers through his hair. "That was great."

Narzek liked that she seemed in no hurry to separate from him. He was content to enjoy their connection until he waned. When he pulled out of her, the condom retracted from his cock, sealing his semen inside it. He then disposed of it in the refuse tube for that purpose.

Then he pulled her close to cuddle her head against the hollow of his shoulder. He realized as he held her that for the first time in more than two years, the ache of loss was almost gone. He found his *solmatu,* and one of his sisters was found. It gave him hope that they would yet find his mother alive.

He closed his eyes with a contented sigh and drifted to sleep.

Cayla had drifted to sleep soon after she laid her head against the hollow of Narzek's shoulder. She woke slowly to his kissing her neck and nibbling her earlobe. The memory of the hard, passionate sex they had shared made her pussy clench with desire. She wanted him again.

She began stroking the back of his head as he was nuzzling her. He raised up and smiled at her, dropping a kiss on her lips. "I want to taste every part of you."

Her nipples went hard, and her core clenched again, and she said, "Mm, that sounds lovely."

Narzek kissed her neck again, where it met her shoulder, nipping her lightly before he dragged his lips down her chest to her breast, nibbling and tasting her. Her nipples seemed to tighten even more with his approach, and she moaned her approval as he dragged his teeth over one hard peak. He took it into his mouth and bit down with just enough pressure to send waves of sensation to her clit.

Those sensations grew more intense as he sucked hard on her nipple. She moaned and squirmed, stroking his head and back. As he moved to her other breast, his hand slid down her belly toward her mons, and she sucked in a breath of anticipation. He pushed a finger in between her nether lips brushing over her clit and into her slick opening.

It seemed like her whole body was sensitized to his touch, and she delighted in his caresses. She murmured his name, sighing and humming while running her hands over him, loving the feel of his smooth skin and taut muscles. She arched her back, pressing her breast against his mouth as he sucked it.

He nipped it just before he released her nipple to drag his delightful mouth down over her ribs. Narzek took his time teasing her moving achingly slow toward her throbbing center.

He parted the dark curls, exposing her swollen center, and blew against it, watching her clench. He pushed up her parted thighs and wrapped his arms around them, holding them apart. Then he lowered his mouth to her clit, stroking it with his tongue. Cayla tried to buck her hips, but Narzek held her fast, driving her wild with pleasure. She had never felt anything so exquisite.

He paused, flicking his tongue over her clit, to slide his tongue into her opening, fucking her with it, and lapping her juices. Then he went back to licking and sucking her clit, sliding two fingers inside her, and thrusting them in and out of her while she clutched at the bedcover, panting and moaning.

Cayla felt like she was floating as the delightful sensations rippled through her body from what Narzek was doing. She reveled in his possession as he drew her closer and closer to that pinnacle of release.

She cried out a series of moans and ahs as the first wave of her orgasm hit her, lifting her hips up off the bed. He kept it going until she shrieked as the intensity became too much. He then laid his head on her belly while her inner walls continue contracting around his fingers. She still bucked her hips intermittently but only moaned and sighed softly.

When she quieted, Narzek withdrew his fingers and licked them clean. Releasing her legs, he wiped his face with his forearm and moved up to lay his head on her breast. Cayla put one hand on his shoulder and caressed his head with the other one while he played with her exposed breast and plucked at her beaded nipple.

She shuddered intermittently with aftershocks of her orgasm.

"I want you again," he murmured and moved to take her nipple in his mouth.

Cayla gasped. "I want you, too."

Narzek released her nipple and reached for another condom.

Cayla was tempted to take him without it but hesitated. Was she really ready to commit to him for life based on a session of mind-blowing sex? She was tempted yet not entirely sure, so she waited and watched the high-tech condom sheath his impressive cock.

Seconds later, she welcomed him inside her as he kissed her deeply. He started thrusting slowly, hard and deep, thrusting his tongue into her mouth in the same rhythm. She loved the feel of him slamming against her with the hilt of his cock rubbing against her clit and his weight pressing down on her breasts. Each thrust caressed her nipples with his hard, muscular chest.

Everything about their joining felt right, like she belonged in his arms, giving and taking pleasure in him. Every time his hips slammed into hers, driving his cock deep, she felt he was claiming her.

She clung to him, sobbing her pleasure as they hurtled to ecstasy together. He seemed to know instinctively what she needed and wanted. Closer and closer until she trembled breathlessly on the brink of rapture until he came, and she sobbed his name as they sailed into completion together.

Chapter Eight

Narzek collapsed on top of her, and Cayla hugged him, stroking his back and head as they panted breathlessly.

"I believe you," she murmured. Cayla realized there was almost no way she could ever walk away from this man. It was more than hot sex; it was nearly spiritual knowing.

"That we are *solmatu*?" He raised himself up on his forearms to look into her eyes.

"Yes," she smiled. Stroking his cheek with her fingers. "I can't explain it; I just know."

Narzek smiled back at her and dropped a light kiss on her lips. "Does that mean you will allow me to claim you as my lifemate?"

"I believe that we are headed in that direction. I'm not going anywhere. This is only the day after we met. In my world, we don't differentiate between what you call sharing sex and claiming."

They kissed and caressed for a while, still joined. It just felt too good to separate until they had to.

Cayla wasn't there yet, but she could see herself falling in love with Narzek. He certainly had a lot going for him; besides that, he was a fantastic lover. When they finally separated, they realized it had been hours since they had eaten.

Narzek found himself staring at Cayla as she picked her clothes up from the floor, naked. That was enough to make him hard all over again. She smiled and quirked an eyebrow at him. Then she grinned.

"That's very tempting, but food first, hanky panky later."

Narzek shrugged. "You are even more beautiful than I could have imagined. And now that we've shared sex, I know how good it feels to be inside you."

Then he smiled, as he noticed her nipples were taut and erect as she was trying not to stare at his fully erect cock. She licked her lips and raised her eyes to his face, and her cheeks flushed a lovely shade of pink. He gave her a sexy smirk, and she turned her back to him and started to pull her shirt on over her head.

Looking at her rounded ass didn't help calm his erection all that much as he imagined cupping those cheeks as he pressed her up against the wall and fucked her hard. He shook his head and tried to clear his mind of sexual thoughts as he bent down to pick up his trousers. Pointedly staring at the beige floor, he pulled them on while thinking about armor maintenance. He retrieved his shirt next and pulled it on over his head. Finally, his cock became flaccid, and he could fasten his pants without the tell-tale bulge.

Narzek didn't doubt that the entire crew knew he had declared *solmatu* by now. While those who reported *solmatu* were given special consideration to have their soulmate aboard a military warship, there were still protocols to follow. Displays of affection or physical intimacy in common areas where they might be observed by other personnel were forbidden.

Not that most men would blame him for becoming aroused by Cayla, especially after the mind-blowing sex they had shared. But despite the fact he was an officer, he was a newbie on this ship. Granted, he was one among many. It was only human nature that some would envy his recent good fortune.

After tucking in his shirt and fastening his trousers, he looked up to see Cayla in front of the closet door mirror, trying to smooth her tousled hair with her fingers. Narzek went to a cupboard door by the bed and took out a plastic brush, and stepped behind her, showing it to her in the mirror.

He handed her the brush and stood watched as she carefully brushed the snarls out of her shoulder-length brown hair.

"We were lucky if we had a comb between us. I usually tied it back to keep it from getting too many tangles. When I was deployed, it was just easier to keep it short."

"Some of our female warriors wear short hair, plait it, or tie it up, so it looks like an animal tail."

"We call them ponytails. A pony is an animal with a tail covered with thick long hair. I could probably do that if I had something to hold it together," Cayla said.

"Praxu display hair restraints available from stores," Narzek said. A short list appeared in the mirror. A round clip, a thin tie, and an inch-wide tube looked like a piece of pipe.

"That one, I think." Cayla pointed to the last one.

"We can stop at the storeroom after our meal to get some as well as a standard grooming kit," he said.

He wanted to wrap his arms around her from behind as he gazed at her image in the mirror. His cock twitched at the thought of holding her, so he didn't.

He rested his hand lightly on her shoulder and said, "Shall we go?"

Cayla nodded and turned to face him. She looked like she might want to hug him, and he took a step back. A slight wrinkle of her brow indicated confusion at the subtle rebuff.

"I really want to hold you, but we won't be able to leave if I do."

"Oh." She gave him a sheepish smile. "Then I guess we better go."

They were late for second meal, as they called the midday meal so there were only a few people in the mess. Since it was all automated, they could get food any time of day to accommodate different shifts. Narzek was off duty for the next several rotations, as were some of the other ground fighters, now that they had completed the extraction from Berrapo. It was up to the ship's operating teams to get them to the next extraction.

His team had nothing to do but train since they had done complete maintenance on their weapons and armor on the way to Berrapo. The overseers and guards were no match for the show of force by the Farseek Brigade. They surrendered without a fight. Some of them even tried to defect. They were denied.

The ground fighters were accustomed to

long periods of downtime between planet falls. During those times, they would cross-train on ship operations and maintenance. It had never happened yet, but they needed to know how to fly the dreadnaught if something happened to the pilots. They also learned to fly the shuttles, especially now that each Dread had an extra shuttle.

"Each of the Farseek Dreads staying in the system gave up one of their three shuttles so we could evacuate our people from slavery faster," Narzek explained as he chose food for both of them.

Even though the processor screens showed what they dispensed, Cayla was not familiar with what the dishes contained.

"So, do you know how to pilot a shuttle?" Cayla asked.

"Yes, I even helped with some of the extraction from Julconi."

"If I am staying with you here, I think I would like to learn shuttle transport. Transportation was my job in the military back home, though that was mostly on the ground."

"That can be quite dangerous," Narzek said. He might have said more, but he heeded her warning look.

"Any military job can be dangerous under

some circumstances, especially in a war zone. I don't even know if I have an aptitude for piloting space shuttles, but it sounds like I will learn if I train to serve in the Brigade. An overheated engine in the desert landed me on an alien slave ship to Berrapo."

"And you came here because of me." Narzek shook his head. "Just being on this ship, we are both in danger. I should have taken you to the *Kurellis* and returned to Farseek with you because I knew I couldn't send you away."

"But you still have three family members to account for," Cayla finished for him.

"Yes. I will understand if you don't want to stay. Your friend will be going to Farseek probably after the next raid," he said, picking up his tray and heading for a table where they would be alone.

"Is that what you want?"

He shook his head as he set his tray down on the side that put his back to the wall. "It's what I should want for your safety; however, I don't know when I might see you again."

"And I think we both know where this is headed. Separating now is unacceptable."

Narzek smiled at her. "Exactly."

Cayla used the hybrid fork-spoon to try a bite of the meat and vegetable medley that he had chosen for her. "Mm. This is pretty good for military food, way better than slave food on Berrapo. It was bland, so it didn't taste horrible, but it didn't taste good either. We ate it because that's all there was."

"Our choices are limited, although there are enough to eat something different for a few rotations before repeating."

The rest of the meal passed pleasantly. Afterward, they got the grooming supplies that Cayla needed and returned to Narzek's cabin.

Chapter Nine

When they returned to Narzek's cabin, about an hour later, he set Cayla's supplies on the table in the dining nook to the right of the door and pulled her into his arms. Claiming her mouth in a deep, hot kiss, he drew her tightly against him. Winding her arms around his neck, she swirled her tongue around his, tasting him as he tasted her.

Though she was a little sore from the unaccustomed sex, she couldn't make herself resist. He just felt so damn good. Somehow, she found herself naked more quickly than seemed possible.

Narzek had removed his shirt and dropped his pants to apply a condom. He lifted her up so she could wrap her legs around him as he pressed her against the wall. By then, she was wet enough that he could slide his cock into her with just a bit of resistance as her inner walls stretched to fit him.

The pain was just enough to heighten the pleasure as he took her hard and fast against the wall. He held her ass cheeks, so her lower back didn't get slammed against the wall with every thrust of his cock.

Cayla reveled in his ardor. She had never been fucked with such fervor, nor had she cum so hard as she screamed in ecstasy. They had been entirely in sync so that they orgasmed together.

Afterward, he held her tightly, pressing his face into her neck where it met her shoulder. Cayla held him tightly, pressing her lips tenderly to his neck.

She didn't think it was possible to fall in love so quickly, but she was undoubtedly infatuated. Sex with him was so good! Only, there was more than just hot sex between them. She liked him. Enough to commit for life? She didn't know.

The next few days went about the same. They ate, slept, and had up to three rounds of sex a day. They couldn't keep their hands off each other whenever they were alone.

On the fourth day, Narzek's sister called through the ship's AI communication network. Azur Pardantu cried when she saw her big brother on the screen.

"Oh, Narz. It is so good to see you. They separated us on the slave ship, so Mom and Jakkin went to different planets, and I don't know which ones."

"Don't worry, Azur, we've just started

looking. We're going to keep looking as long as we can. There is a new house on our family property, waiting for you when you get back to Farseek. You'll be headed there as soon as we fill the *Kurellis*.

"But I will be there alone."

"My friends Kragyn and Argen are there with their *solmatus*. I will let them know you are coming. There are also people from other worlds settling on Farseek. We rescued everyone who had been enslaved who wanted to come. Some were dropped off on other worlds, but many came to Farseek."

"I wish I could come with you."

"No, you don't. Every system we stop in Sargan loyalist battleships could be waiting. I don't even want my *solmatu* to be here, but she was a warrior on her world."

"You have a *solmatu?*

"Yes, I found her on Berrapo. Her friend Luanne Field was rescued from there as well. She is on your ship."

"Luanne? I know her. She was in our workgroup but in another barrack. We're friends. Who is your *solmatu?*"

"Cayla Fox."

"Yes! Luanne told me about her. She will be so pleased that Cayla is safe. Is she there with you now?"

"She is. Cayla, come, let me introduce

you to Azur."

Cayla moved into the camera view and smiled at Azur. She was a prettier version of Narzek, the same coloring, hair eyes, face shape, and feminine.

"I am pleased to meet you."

"Me, too. Next time I call, I will have Luanne with me. Narzek, since our house, has been rebuilt, can I invite Luanne to stay with me?"

"I think that would be great for you to have company," he agreed. "I'm sure even if we find the others, they would agree, at least until Luanne figures out how she will support herself. When we come back to Farseek, we will probably build a home of our own."

They talked a few more minutes before Azur ran out of time. With so many people trying to connect with friends and relatives, they were only allotted a few minutes to talk. They were instead encouraged to send text messages because they transmitted so much faster.

Narzek was smiling when the call ended, and so was Cayla, even though she didn't get to speak with her friend. He took her into his arms and kissed the top of her head as he held her.

"It shouldn't be much longer before you

get to speak to your friend. They are probably giving priority to family members just now."

"It's okay. I am just happy to know Luanne is alive and rescued, she said. "I think my language upload is taking effect. I can read the signs now, and I don't get that delay between when you talk and what I understand anymore."

"Then, it's time to get you a com-tablet. The teams are going to start training for landfall at Mecstar Prime. Dread Six is doing recon, and there is more armed security than we found on Berrapo."

"Why do you think that is? What's Mecstar Prime?"

"Energy crystal mining. These are the energy crystals we use to power our starships. That makes them a prime war target," Narzek said. "The Consortium forces are holding off for us to extract the slaves. We must take out the guards before that can happen. They estimate there are at least 2000 Uatu people and another 2000 various humanoid men and women."

"Can I train, too?" Cayla asked.

"I think that can be arranged, but there is no way you will be fully trained in time for this mission."

"I don't expect that. I just figured I have to start someplace. I expect to do more observing at first."

"Praxu, please send a new com-tablet to my cabin for my solmatu Cayla Fox."

"Acknowledged. Order accepted." The computer responded."

"Are you still thinking of becoming a shuttle pilot?"

"Yes, I want to explore the possibility. You said everyone is cross-trained in both starship operations and ground combat," Cayla said. "I did some flying of small aircraft back on Earth because my Uncle George has a small plane with his own landing strip."

"That experience should come in handy on Farseek. We used hover-flyers to get around because there are no roads between our towns and cities."

"Now, that sounds intriguing. Flying cars. Earth never got that far. Our cars have wheels, and there are roads everywhere."

"Some of the older colonies have roads. When Farseek was colonized, flying transport was the most economical way to go." Narzek put his hand under her chin, tilting it upward, contemplating her parted lips. "This is my last rotation off for several; I think we should take advantage of the rest of my free time."

"Whatever do you have in mind?" she

teased, moving her body wantonly against his.

Narzek slid one hand down over her ass and pressed his hardon blatantly against her belly. He took her mouth in a heated, tongue tangling kiss. Before he finished, a two-tone signal alerted him that the delivery he requested had arrived. He reluctantly ended their kiss and released her.

"Enter," he said.

A droid cart rolled into his sitting room bearing the requested com-tablet. Narzek lifted the tablet from the droid. "Now, you just need to apply your thumbprint to the reader; you will be entered into the communications directory, so your friend or anyone else in our fleet may contact you directly."

Cayla complied, and Narzek handed the tablet to her. It looked much like a cell phone. "How does it work?"

"It's voice-activated. Just say what you want. You can ask to speak to a specific person, or you can access AI Praxu's databases for any educational materials you need. All of our operations manuals and job descriptions, and education requirements are available from the AI."

"That's easy enough. And this can even project holograms?"

"Yes, but we can go through all that later,

can't we?"

"I think so." Cayla set her new tablet on the table and turned back to Narzek, sliding her hands up over his chest and around his neck. As they kissed, he subtly moved them into the bedroom.

Narzek kissed and caressed her at length, telling her with his body how much she meant to him. He built her arousal to a fever pitch before he joined them as one. Even then, he drew out their pleasure as long as possible.

Hc had hoped by now to claim her formally as his lifemate, but solmatu didn't affect alien humans as quickly as with the Uatu people. Each time they shared sex, he wanted to claim her, but he had promised to wait until she was ready.

Chapter Ten

A few weeks later, Cayla sighed as she lay spooned against Narzek in the bed they now shared. He cuddled her against him with one arm around her, cupping his hand over her breast. Though he never asked in words, she knew he was bidding with every kiss, every caress, every thrust of his cock deep inside her. He was asking to claim her as a *solmatu* bond mate.

She believed she was falling in love with him. What was not to love about the smoking hot Farseek warrior? She couldn't imagine a better lover or lifemate. Committing to becoming Narzek's lifemate meant it was unlikely she would ever go back to Earth. Going back to Earth would mean likely never seeing Narzek again.

As she thought of saying goodbye to Narzek forever, a lump swelled in her throat, and tears filled her eyes. The tears spilled over and wet her pillow, and she curved her hand over his that still cupped her breast. There was only one viable choice. She knew the first time he kissed her, there would be nothing casual about their relationship.

Cayla wept softly, choking back her sobs so as not to wake him. Only, Narzek was not sleeping as soundly as she thought; she couldn't suppress the shudder that passed through her body that woke him.

"Hey, sweetheart, what is it?" he whispered near her ear.

"Sorry, I didn't mean to wake you. I know you are on duty tomorrow," she sniffed. "I just realized I can't go back to Earth without you, and that means I will probably never go back and see my parents again. They are sure to think I am dead after all this time."

Cayla turned over to face him, unable to stop crying. Narzek kissed her forehead and held her, letting her cry it out while he rubbed her back and stroked her silky hair.

"What are you trying to tell me, Cay?" he asked finally.

"I accept you as my mate. But that's not why I was crying." She sniffed. "It was when I thought of never seeing you again that it started. Then I thought about never seeing Earth or Mom and Dad again. Even if I went back, I couldn't stay there without you."

"So, you want me to claim you?" He cupped his hand to her cheek and stared into her eyes in the dim blue night light.

"Yes." She gave him a tender smile.

"Now?"

She nodded. "You know we won't sleep until you do." Besides, his cock went hard when he pulled her against him, which of course, made her wet for him as it nestled against her core.

Narzek rolled her beneath him, his hips between her legs, kissing her and teasing her tongue with his. Cayla hugged and caressed him as he kissed her, tilting her pelvis so her wet slit rubbed against his cock.

As the kiss went on, Cayla reached between them and gripped his cock. He raised his hips, and she drew the head up her channel and poised it to slide into her. He sank it into her balls deep without ever breaking the kiss, but he never started pumping in and out of her until their lips parted, and he could look her in the eyes as he claimed her.

Cayla smiled up at him and stared into his eyes; she knew instinctively he desired it. It was their most intense mating yet because it was claiming sex.

Narzek started slowly, drawing his cock outward in a slow caress of her inner walls and driving it back into her, rotating his hips to rub the hilt against her clit. Each time he thrust into her, Cayla gave a little moan of pleasure. He kept his steady pace drawing her pleasure slowly toward the mutual ecstasy they always found when they shared sex.

She murmured his name breathlessly as her arousal increased to where she could sense her orgasm building. He dropped his head to kiss her again and started thrusting harder and faster, slipping his tongue into her mouth in that same rhythm.

Cayla made mewing sounds of pleasure and pressed her fingertips into his back as her muscles tightened and her breath came faster. She felt Narzek's muscles tighten under her fingers as he pounded into her. Later she would tell him it was the best fucking she ever had.

She moaned urgently, and Narzek tore his mouth from hers. Throwing back his head, he let out a roar of triumph as he came and pumped his semen into her womb. She cried out at the same time, digging her fingernails into his back with the intensity of her climax.

After the first surge of their release, they fixed their gazes on each other as they surged and waned, panting from the exertion. Narzek lowered himself against her but held most of his weight on his forearms.

"I am yours, and you are mine as long as I draw breath," Narzek repeated the *solmatu* claiming oath.

Cayla raised her hands to his cheeks as she continued to hold his gaze. "I am yours, and you are mine as long as I draw breath," she repeated back to him. "This happened way faster than I thought possible. I'm not even sure how this is going to work, but you made me a believer. We are *solmatu*, and I love you."

"And I love you." He gave her a soft, sweet kiss on her lips.

That was how romances Cayla once read would end, but this was nowhere near the end of their story. Somehow, someday she still needed to let her parents know she was still alive out there among the stars. She couldn't ignore the fact that they were on a dangerous mission, and they could all be killed. Worse, one of them could die, and the other left to go on with their life alone.

Of course, she could have been killed at her job in that desert warzone back on Earth without the chance of loving a man like Narzek. Aside from her relationship with him, she also felt like she owed the Farseek Brigade for freeing her from slavery. They didn't pick and choose which people to rescue who were enslaved on Berrapo. They took every being who wanted to take their offer of freedom.

The Uatu people from Farseek valued

their freedom above wealth and prosperity. Farm life on Farseek gave most people a comfortable living. Working the land and growing things on a world with fertile soil and a climate with long growing seasons was everything the Uatu people hoped for when they settled there many star orbits before Narzek or Cayla were born.

There was no revenge that they could take against Evzen Guryon that would repay him for the heinous thing he did in orchestrating the Sargan attack on Farseek. The only way Cayla could repay the Farseek Brigade for her freedom was to help them free more of their people. She had already decided she would serve any way she could be of help.

Despite his shortage of sleep, Narzek was in a great mood when he strode into the training room for unarmed combat practice. It was more an exercise to keep their reflexes sharp and maintain physical conditioning. Depending on the mission, they used six to ten member teams.

Narzek's team was comprised of seven men and two women. Most of them were transfers from other Dreadnaughts, so most of them didn't have to establish friendships with each other. Since they had been assigned to serve under him, they had developed a sense of comradery and cooperation.

The team first went through stretching exercises and endurance training on their high-tech treadmills, then weight training. Then they were ready for hand-to-hand sparring matches.

All disciplined professionals who knew how to work as a team, they drew lots for sparring partners.   Narzek drew Seronna Brevatu, one of the female members of his team. It didn't matter that she was female; they were all trained to the expert level in *Fehiatu,* the Uatu ancient martial arts. Many had started the training as children even before they were required to begin warrior training.

What Seronna lacked in upper body strength, she made up in skill. Narzek knew better than to consider her an easy win. In two out of three rounds, each won one, and they tied for the third.

Their training session finished well past the usual time for second meal, but Narzek called Cayla to join him after he showered and   changed.

Chapter Eleven

Cayla had meant to get up when Narzek rose for his scheduled training session, but he had urged her to sleep a little longer. She still felt tired and a little drained emotionally now that she had made her decision. She could only believe that he must bc hcr soul mate because the thought of leaving him and never seeing him again caused her so much pain.

She got up slowly, feeling a little achy from the sexual workout they had shared. A quick hot shower help ease that soreness. But it was worth it, she thought, to see the joy in Narzek's eyes as he claimed her. By the time she had emerged from the bathroom to dress, the bunk she had shared with him had made itself.

Cayla was not very hungry, so she got a cup of tea from the dispenser in the wall by the table in their cabin and ate a protein bar from the rack also on the wall. While she ate, she opened her tablet and asked for the qualifications to become a member of the Farseek Brigade. Even with her own military training, she still had much to learn because of the cross-training and high-tech weapons.

At least she did have martial arts training. She had started karate lessons when she was a kid. The *fehiatu* practiced by the Farseek Brigade was more similar than different. Because she was thinking about learning to fly shuttles, she also looked up the requirements for that. Apparently, flying small planes back on Earth only qualified her to pilot transport flyers planet side. That only meant she would need more training. The first step would be aptitude testing.

Now that her language module had been assimilated, she could not only speak the common Consortium language of the Farseekans, but she could read it as well. There was still time for her to start the testing before the next planetfall. Cayla wanted to check with Narzek's schedule so they could spend his free time together.

Cayla had just started learning about the Farseek planet when Narzek called to ask her to join him for a late second meal. She was just a little nervous about meeting his team. Narzek waited for her in the corridor outside the mess hall, apparently anticipating her discomfort.

He greeted her with a warm smile and took her hand as she came to face him. Cayla smiled back as he gave her hand an affectionate squeeze, then let go as they entered the mess together. Some of his team members were still in the food line, making their selections as they progressed through the self-serve bar.

Narzek and Cayla joined the line and took their turn choosing their food as they progressed. They sat with his team at one of the long tables in the dining area. Two seats at the head of the table had been left open for them. Setting down his tray, he called for their attention, which they gave immediately.

"This is Cayla Fox of Earth, my bond-mate and *solmatu*. She is a trained warrior from her world, and she wishes to join us. Like so many of our people, Cayla was abducted from her world and enslaved by the Sargans."

Then he introduced his team, starting with Seronna Brevatu, in the seat beside Cayla's. He went on to name each one of them: Covron Lagatu, Weglan Kopatu, Bendar Sakitu, Prunat Melistu, Ebna Zaykentu, Baxar Kiatu, Kierton Fedotu, Dias Elatu. Serrona and Dias were the female members of the team. They nodded in turn as they were introduced.

Cayla repeated each name to herself so that she would remember them. Remembering names and details was an essential skill for a soldier from any world. As a driver in a warzone, it was crucial for her survival and that of her passengers to notice details that might prove a danger to her and per passengers.

No one ever told her to watch out for extraterrestrial alien slavers. Getting abducted by aliens was the thing that never crossed her mind, while she worried about roadside bombs and ambushes by hostiles.

Cayla mentally shook herself as she looked at each member of Narzek's team. They were literally a colorful bunch. Skin tones varied from her mate's bluish lavender to blue-gray, brighter blue, mahogany, and dark blue-black with hair in neon colors. Even before she met them, Narzek assured her that they were all genetically human.

Seronna, who sat beside her, was blue with cropped red hair and beautiful. Cayla imagined she looked almost as unusual to his team as they looked at her with her pale skin and brown hair. The other female sitting across from her was a darker shade of lavender than Narzek with pink hair.

Both of them smiled at Cayla as she sat down.

"It's always nice to have another female join us," said Seronna. "We have heard of

Earth from our first mission to recover some of our people. Dread One had four females from Earth join them."

"Then they rescued a Narovian feline who was from the United Galactic Alliance in the same sector as Earth," Dias added.

"They rescued a female feline from Julconi, and she put Dread Four in contact with the Alliance. They, in turn, routed messages to Earth about the Earthers they rescued," said Bendar. "Communications should be able to relay a message to your people. It's a little tricky because our systems don't exactly mesh, but it can be done."

"Narzek has mentioned it, but with all the communications from the *Kurellis* being relayed. We decided to wait. And I was still deciding whether to stay."

"I won't ask what changed your mind," said Dias. "I've seen the way you look at LC. Since you are *solmatu*, you aren't required to accept formal duties."

"Yes, Narzek told me, but I need to contribute. On my world, we have a practice called pay it forward. Your people saved me from life as a slave. I can't exactly return the favor, but I can help in some way to rescue other people facing the same fate."

"Cayla plans to take our general aptitude

tests to see what type of work she is suited for," Narzek said.

"Even then, I will still have to train. In the meantime, I will keep up my physical training. I'm trying to talk LC here into letting me join your sparring matches."

"Do you know *fehiatu?*" asked Seronna.

"I learned something called karate. That means 'empty hand.' It seems like it would be comparable."

"That might be fun to try. We don't usually do full contact anyway," said Dias. "We don't want to have anyone seriously injured before a mission."

The team talked among themselves and asked Cayla questions about Earth. Narzek didn't always attend meals with his team, but he wanted Cayla to have a chance to meet the team he worked with and possibly make some new friends.

A few days later, Cayla finally got to have a video talk with her friend Luanne. "You look good, Cay. Azur tells me that you are mated to her brother."

"Yeah, we are soul mates. They call it *solmatu.* I didn't quite believe it at first. I didn't plan to stay, but I couldn't bear the thought of never seeing Narzek again," Cayla told her. "Farseek is a beautiful world; at least it was before the Sargan's ruined it. But a lot of it has been rebuilt. Did you see the pictures of their new family home?"

"I did. I've accepted Azur's invitation to live there until I find a place to settle. We were told there would be refugee housing," Luanne said. "I don't see me going back to Earth. I don't have any family, nobody waiting for me. Maybe I will find someone to settle with and make a family someday."

"We plan to return to Farseek if all goes well," Cayla said. "Narzek wants to keep looking for the rest of his family as long as the Brigade will keep at it."

"But the war with the Sargans has started back up. The Sargan Starfleet refuses to recognize the authority of the Consortium or the Alliance. We're still in a warzone."

Cayla chuckled. "At least we are free. Anyway, there was no guarantee we would come back from that warzone back on Earth. We owe these Sargans for enslaving us in the first place. We weren't the first or the last taken from Earth to become slaves."

"You're right. The Sargans need to be stopped. I kind of wish I'd ended up on one of the warships," Luanne said.

"And I wish it would be this one. I've really missed you, Lu."

"Me   too,   Cay."

Chapter Twelve

Narzek's relationship with Cayla continued to blossom. Cayla's aptitude testing showed that she could make a good shuttle pilot with training, plus a talent for communications. Cayla would train as a pilot, but it could take half a sun rotation or more for her to be ready to pilot shuttles from orbit to the planet.

While she was studying math and astrophysics, she would need to become a space shuttle pilot, the commander in charge assigned her to shuttle maintenance. Even though they used droids to do a lot of the scut work, they still use pilots and trainees to run system checks.

Cayla was happy to have the assignment. Having flown small planes on Earth, she knew how essential proper maintenance was. The technology of the basic transport shuttles was beyond anything they had on Earth. It made her feel useful and allowed her to make new friends.

She also got to participate in some sparring matches with Narzek's team. He practiced with her at first to see how her martial arts training compared to *fehiatu*. Narzek determined that karate was indeed comparable to *fehiatu*.

Although Narzek was not unusually a jealous man, he requested that Cayla only sparred with the women on his team because they used a semi-contact technic. Cayla might have taken offense had he forbidden sparring with the other men. He asked her not to because he didn't feel he could watch another man pretending to attack her. As a concession to fairness, Narzek didn't spar with the women.

Both of the women had official bond mates who were in starship operations which were *solmatu*. During off-duty times, Narzek and Cayla socialized with them, among others.

Even with Cayla in training, most of what they did from one day to the next was to fill the time until the next mission. The best part of those days was when they were off duty in the privacy of their quarters. Aside from their passionate sexual relationship, their emotional connection grew as they shared their pasts and hopes for the future.

As far as Cayla could calculate in time, it would take them a month and a half to reach the Mecstar system. Several rotations before they blinked into that star system, the officers held briefing sessions for the landing teams and the shuttle pilots.

Reconnaissance showed minimal activity by the Sargans within the system. Still, they were mostly freighters hauling the crystals to distribute to their manufacturing facilities, spaceports, and space stations where ships might stop to have their worn crystals replaced.

If they filled the *Kurellis* as they hoped from this planet, they would need to find another transport for their next mission. Though the freighters weren't ideal, they were the only other ships they might successfully seize for that purpose. A Sargan battleship would be large enough to carry a few thousand souls, but they didn't have the manpower to subdue the thousands of crewmembers necessary to take control.

They were better equipped to destroy a battlecruiser than to commandeer one.

Both Narzek and Cayla were feeling the stress of the upcoming mission, but for different reasons. Narzek felt confident his team was ready for the planetfall. Even so, there could be surprises to muck things up.

Dreadnaught Six and Eight had jumped ahead of their tiny fleeted to land teams on

Mecstar Prime to gather intel to work out the logistics of how many they needed to extract from the planet. Between the mine sites and the processing plants, there were more than four thousand Uatu to rescue. There were hundreds of other humans and humanoids that needed to be saved as well.

The recon teams were charged with recruiting the Uatu people to help organize their brethren and get them to the predetermined pickup sites. Even if all the evacuees were ready and waiting at the landing sites, they could take each shuttle six to seven trips from the ground to the Kurellis to evacuate everyone who wanted to leave.

They had learned how to streamline the processes during their first rescue mission. Rescuing three to four thousand people would still be a lengthy process. Two of the dreadnaughts were put into orbit around Mecstar Prime. They sent six ground combat teams to the biggest mining operations to reconnoiter a few days before the rest of the dreadnaughts and the *Kurellis* arrived.

Once the first teams landed, the Dreads Six and Eight pulled out of Mecstar Prime orbit and moved to Mecstar Tertiary to hide in stealth mode while the ground teams did their work. More teams would land when the rest of the dreads arrived to neutralize the overseers and guards. Whether they lived or died depended on whether they surrendered or fought.

Not until the final days of Dreadnaught Ten's approach to the Mecstar system did Cayla begin to fret about Narzek's safety during his mission ground side on Prime. So many things could go wrong, and they could all be in danger if any Sargan battleships blinked in on patrol. The worst part is that Cayla knew she would be stuck on their ship doing scut work for the shuttle crews.

She didn't mind the scut work; it was waiting for Narzek to complete his mission and return, so she knew he was safe. His team had trained daily in the holographic training compartment. He did this more for team building rather than just honing their skills.

Every member of the Farseek Brigade was the best of the best. Other Earthers called them Army Rangers, Navy Seals, Marines, and Black Ops rolled into one. The Farseek Brigade was known for its aggressive combat skills and raw courage throughout the Consortium. If anyone could do what they were planning, they could.

After the Sargan attack on Farseek, the Brigade had felt betrayed by the Consortium. They believed the Consortium orchestrated the attack, not just one man. Cayla learned from her studies that the Consortium High Council put their best investigator on the case to determine who was really behind the attack.

Evzen Guryon was a member of the high council at the time and voted for the investigation. That was how confident he was that his involvement would never be discovered. But in the trail of dead bodies his conspiracy left, there was someone important enough for their loved one to tenaciously follow that trail until they found the source. That person teamed up with the Consortium Investigator to bring Guryon down.

Yet, none of that erased the damage done to over a million people. Every member of the brigade lost friends or family in the attack. That didn't mean they hadn't planned carefully. Getting their people back safely was the top priority. People could still get hurt, even killed.

That it could be Narzek terrified Cayla when she let herself think about the possibility. The nagging uncertainty increased the intensity of their lovemaking. Every time their bodies came together in passion, there was an urgency that these could be their last days together. They made love the last time a day and a half before the mission.

Cayla finished duty before Narzek and used the time to freshen up with a shower. She had donned one of Narzek's t-shirts instead of the robe, which wasn't a standard issue. He arrived to find her bent over her lowest drawer picking out a fresh shirt and pants to wear to the evening meal.

She heard their cabin door whoosh open, so she wasn't surprised when he came up and wrapped his arms around her from behind. He cupped her breast with one hand and kissed her neck as he pulled her against him. She tilted her head back, resting it on his shoulder.

Cayla hummed in pleasure as she gave herself into his caresses. His erection pressing against her buttocks alerted her to his intentions. While kissing her neck and shoulders, he pushed up the t-shirt to cover her bare breasts with his hands. He plucked at her nipples until they stiffened into taut, hard peaks.

Cayla moaned, enjoying his caresses as ripples of sensation ebbed and flowed, making her core throb and clench with desire. He slid a finger over her mons and into her wet slit. He wet the tip with her juices and rubbed it over her clit while pinching her nipple and nipping her shoulder where it met her neck.

He did that until she was squirming and pressing her ass against his hard cock over his pants. Narzek took her hands and placed them against the cupboard door and had her bend at the waist, and spread her legs. She heard the hook loop closure on his trousers pulled open. Then the head of his cock pressed against her slick entrance.

"Is this what you want?" he asked.

"You know it is," she asserted.

Chapter Thirteen

Cayla braced herself for the exquisite pleasure of his cock, filling her. Even though she was slick and ready, it was still a delectably tight fit, so, when he thrust into her, he hit all the right places.

She cried out as he took her, holding her hips to keep from pushing her into the cabinet door.

"I've been thinking about this all day," he said, taking her in slow, deep thrusts, hard enough to make his balls slap against her clit. "Nothing I have done has felt as good as putting my cock into you."

Each phrase was punctuated by another deep thrust that rammed the head against her cervix and hit that inner sweet spot.

"Yes," was the most coherent thing she could say in response to the intensity of sensation that made her catch her breath in gasps and moans.

Narzek paused, still inside her, and slid his hands under her shirt, squeezing and needing her breasts and pinching her taut nipples. Cayla cooed her approval and clenched his cock with her inner walls. He kissed and nipped at her neck while he continued teasing her nipples with his fingers.

He did that until Cayla was on the verge of her first orgasm, and then he stopped. She let out a frustrated groan, but her distress was short-lived as he straightened to start pumping in and out of her harder and faster.

Cayla braced herself even as he held on to her hips as he rammed his cock into her. Every stroke brought her closer and closer to that pinnacle of ecstasy that she had only ever found with Narzek.

He fucked her hard with the fiercest passion she had ever experienced. She not only loved it, but she craved it; she craved him.

Like him, she had gone about her day, unable to stop her mind from wandering to when they could be together and do this again.

For a time, there were only the sounds of their slight grunts and moans and the slapping together of their flesh. Closer and closer, in her mind's eye she flew higher and higher toward her climax. As it built low in her belly, her muscles tensed and she breathed in short shallow gasps.

She keened as the first contraction hit her, and her channel squeezed against his thrusting cock. Her body jerked with her release but Narzek barely slowed.

Cayla wasn't worried, because it was only the first orgasm of a few or several that he would elicit from her.

Time seemed to stand still as she held herself steady for Narzek's driving thrusts. Cayla came twice more before he found his release, and then she came yet again as he roared, pouring his seed into her womb. Her body jerked, and shuddered with each throb of his cock inside.

This time, Narzek thrust slowly in and partly out of her, teasing her through her final orgasm. She cooed and hummed blissfully as it played out at length.

When it finally ended, Narzek leaned over her, still inside her and wrapped his arms around her in a tender hug. "That was so good." He pressed his lips to the back of her neck, then cupped her breasts, kneading them lightly, causing an aftershock of her orgasm that pleasured him even more.

Some mini-spans later, he finally, reluctantly pulled out of her, his erection spent. As they straightened, Cayla turned around and pressed herself against him. "I love you." *And I am scared.*

She didn't dare give voice to the last,

because she thought it could somehow jinx their mission. When she looked into Narzek's eyes, she knew he felt it too.

"I love you, too, my *solmatu.*" He tilted her face up and lowered his mouth to hers in a deep, tender kiss, extending his tongue into her mouth to caress hers in a sweet, slow dance. It seemed almost that he was making it up to her for fucking her without a kiss. But it was too good for her to really mind.

After that long, slow kiss, they just held each other for a while.

"We should get cleaned up." Narzek released her gradually. "Do you mind if we eat in rather than at the mess hall?"

"I never mind having you all to myself." She smiled at him. If this were to be the last night they would ever have together, she wasn't going to spoil it with the fears nagging the back of her mind.

Narzek toed off his boots and stepped out of his cargo pants, then picked them up from the floor to take out his com tablet. He ordered their food by the touch screen then set it on the shelf by the cabinet door, stripping off his t-shirt.

Cayla did the same and went into the shower ahead of him. It was a tight fit but there was just enough room. As he put his arms around her, his hard cock pressed into her belly. She looked up at him unable to suppress a smile. "Again?"

He grinned back, his familiar sexy smirk and lifted her up so she could wrap her legs around his waist. Pressing her against the wall, he slid his cock into her and proceeded to fuck her again, kissing her long and slow. It was much later that they showered and dressed for dinner.

Even after dinner, Narzek would have made love to her again. It was not unusual for them to couple far into the night, particularly while they were en route to their mission. All the ground forces were on light duty until the last six rotations. They trained hard and reviewed all the intel and aerial stills of the mining sites, the slave barracks and the number of hostiles that might hinder them from getting their people back.

He had studied the layout and committed it to memory. Their plans were simple. It was the same technic the Brigade used when they turned mercenary, thinking the Consortium had betrayed them.

Their body armor gave them the power of cybernetics externally. It gave them clear night vision and augmented their physical strength. The night vision was crucial to the mission because they went in after dark in stealth mode and neutralized the guards and overseers. That would be the easy part.

Most of the security in the facilities they shut down in the past were not trained warriors with state-of-the-art weapons. There was no evidence that these hostiles were any better armed. Narzek was not concerned with the danger of his mission. He was more worried that he wouldn't find his other family members.

Being well rested for the mission was part of his duty to his team and the brigade. He had learned early on in his career to clear his mind and relax his body so he could sleep. It was a technic that they practiced. Cayla had learned meditation that worked similarly.

It was going to be a long grueling operation with twenty shuttles going back and forth from the *Kurellis*. The evacuation teams would stay on the ground until every last slave was extracted from Medstar Prime. It would take most of three shifts to get the job done.

Soon after they dined, they went to bed and cuddled together spoon fashion until they drifted into a deep, dreamless sleep.

The next morning, they woke a few mini-spans before the ship's AI was to wake them. It wasn't unusual for them to wake early to have sex before they started their day. Narzek wanted Cayla as much as always, but they both knew it wasn't to be this morning. He was duty bound to conserve his energy for the mission.

Instead, after a trip to the bathroom, they just held each other, kissing and caressing until the alarm sounded. Then they dressed and went to morning meal with the rest of the ground teams.

Following the meal, Narzek reported to the armory to suit up in body armor before transport groundside to Mecstar Prime. Narzek could see that Cayla wanted to hug him one more time, but settled for clasping hands.

"See you when you get back," Cayla said softly.

He merely nodded and gave her hands a gentle squeeze. Cayla turned abruptly as he released her and strode toward the landing bay without looking back.

Narzek watched with a wry grin, thinking of how they would celebrate when he got back.

Chapter Fourteen

Although it was morning for the Farseek Brigade Dreadnaughts standing by in the Mecstar system, it was evening and dark for most of their targets on Mecstar Prime. The recon teams moved in to secure the barracks in their sections. By doing so, they could roust out those enslaved to be ready to load the shuttles bringing down reinforcements as soon as they were emptied.

Narzek's team was assigned to secure Mine Site #3 and guide the slaves to the shuttle landing coordinates. Meanwhile, their shuttle would move to the closest barracks with people ready for transport. Their show of force put fear into the guards and overseers armed with low-tech projectile rifles and pistols as he had hoped.

They seemed to know their weapons wouldn't phase fully armored professional warriors. Most of them surrendered, and some of them fled. It was time-consuming to scan the different tunnels to find all of the slaves laboring there.

Enough Farseekans were among them

who recognized the insignias on their armor to help calm the others and tell them the armed invaders were there to rescue them. As word spread through the workers, they left their hammers and chisels and headed for the mine entrance to await shuttle pick up.

They locked the Sargan henchmen, and women who surrendered were into an office while the freed slaves were collected to wait for the shuttles. There were a little over three hundred people at that mine location. The troop shuttles were designed to hold about thirty people with a fairly large cargo capacity.

By filling the cargo bay with people sitting on the floor, they could carry a hundred or so people in one trip. Narzek's team waited with them once they were assembled near the landing coordinates until everyone was transported. Other squads had more people to move in the larger mining sites, so Narzek commandeered a hover tram and took his team to the next location to help find the workers in the maze of tunnels.

The entire operation went more smoothly than they expected. Since they finished evacuations in the primary objectives, they moved on to secondary locations where less than a hundred slaves might be located.

Narzek was determined to root out every slave he could because even if they weren't his family members, he didn't want to leave any Farseekans behind by overlooking them. Six large mining sites used hundreds of slaves for the equivalent of ten-hour shifts.

There were at least ten smaller sites where twenty to fifty slaves were working. Those teams not supervising the extraction of the rescues from the six main sites were dispatched to the secondary sites. It made for a long day, but their efforts yielded another thousand slaves free.

Things were going better than expected. Aside from their show of force against the Sargan keepers, they might have just been picking up passengers. It just felt too easy to Narzek, and he got that same feeling coming from his other team members.

Cayla spent most of the day on standby at the conference room off the landing bay in case any of the shuttles might return for maintenance or repair. The landing bay doors remained opened with a force field holding the atmosphere inside. From the large window in the conference room, she could see stars and open space.

While she paused to gaze out into space from time to time, she spent most of the hours studying the operating manual for the shuttles she wanted to learn to fly. Some of the other maintenance workers watched other things on their tablets to pass the time.

Dreadnaught Ten was in orbit over one of Mecstar Prime's smaller moons. Something in Cayla's peripheral vision made her look toward the space outside the landing bay. A Sargan Battle Carrier suddenly blinked into space Within striking distance from the Dread Ten, and space fighters started pouring from its launch bays.

At least three fighters were coming toward the dreadnaught's landing bay. Cayla's supervisor Hykara Elbatu saw them at the same time.

"Everybody out the back door, NOW!" she shouted. "Return to your quarters and stay there until further notice. Do not use the lifts!"

All ten of them jumped up from their seats and hurried to the exit in an orderly fashion while Hykara waited beside the open door for everyone to leave. As Cayla glanced back, the heavily shielded landing bay doors slammed shut on the approaching fighters.

An alarm was blaring intermittently as they walked the sublevel corridor toward the ladder tubes past the lifts.

They had trained for this. Starship operation personnel had precedence over maintenance workers in emergency situations. So, Cayla's team waited patiently for their turn in the ladder tubes. There was a railing along the hallway for them to anchor so they wouldn't be slammed to the floor when weapons fire shook the ship in an attack.

Cayla tensed as the ship shuddered with the first volley, but she didn't panic. That motion meant that the shields were holding fast. That meant no hull breeches. She could just imagine being stuck inside one of the lifts when they rerouted power to the shields and weapons.

She wasn't crazy about using the ladder tubes; they were a bit claustrophobic, and she had to climb from the sublevel to Level Three to get to hers and Narzek's quarters. Her physical training required her to make that climb every few rotations. She could now climb up the metal ladder with its flat, narrow steps as fast as the rest of the crew.

Fans at the top and bottom of the tubes recirculated their air which helped to keep them from getting overheated as they did the climb.

Once Cayla emerged onto her level, she walked briskly to her cabin. Inside, she climbed into their bunk and pulled out the harness to strap herself in. She took deep, calming breaths, closing her eyes. There was nothing for her to do but wait it out.

The crew quarters were well shielded in the center of the ship. Even if the ship became disabled and sustained hull breeches, the odds were high that the people in their quarters would survive. But Cayla was unsure if she wanted to survive only to be forced back into slavery; or if Narzek didn't make it back to her. She put a stop to those thoughts right away. What if negative thoughts could attract the exact worst-case scenario she feared the most.

The Farseek Brigade was the best of the best; they would fight long and hard. They would die fighting before they would let anyone take their ships.

For now, Narzek was safe on the ground. The updates they'd been getting throughout the day said all was going well ground side. She resigned herself to the fact that there was nothing she could do about what was happening. Instead of just lying there alone in their bed, letting her fears take hold, she closed her eyes then quieted her mind to meditate on the vision she and Narzek shared for the future.

It was just as well that she couldn't see what was happening outside the ship. Ten Sargan battleships blinked into the Mecstar system while they were still shuttling people up to the *Kurellis*. Narzek's team and the others had discovered almost a thousand more people who needed to be evacuated.

That was about five hundred more than the *Kurellis* was designed to carry. Most of the rescued people didn't care if they had to double up in the cabins or sleep in conference rooms or even the cargo bay. Their freedom was worth it.

Two dreadnaughts fought valiantly against four Sargan battle ships and assorted fighters to hold them back from capturing the *Kurellis*. They also protected the shuttles that arrived about every twenty minutes to deposit people on the huge passenger ship.

Before they'd left Farseek for this mission, their shuttles were retrofitted with laser cannons to ward off space fighters from the battle carrier. When they failed to enter any of the dreadnaughts through their landing bays, the fighters turned on the shuttles.

Meanwhile, the dreadnaughts flanking the *Kurellis* kept moving about to block the battle cruisers and fighters from accessing it. The dreadnaughts may have been outnumbered, but the Sargan ships were outgunned.

Multiple one- and two-man fighters broke off and flew lower in attempts to shoot down the evacuation shuttles.

Apparently, it didn't matter whether they killed innocents or not. They were bent on disabling or destroying the shuttles that were stealing their slaves. Many of the enemy fighters were disabled or destroyed during those attacks. One shuttle was forced to go back to the planet before reaching the *Kurellis* to deposit their passengers.

The veteran pilot could make a rough landing, but there were injuries to the passengers, and he hadn't had time to assess them. Their shuttle was not so lucky as it split open as it skidded to a stop in the dirt.

Chapter Fifteen

The dreadnaughts disabled three of the Sargan battle ships and many fighters. They were on the verge of taking out a fourth battle cruiser when three more blinked into the system. The dreads were taking a beating, and their power reserves were being depleted. Their shields could fail, and their weapons were losing power.

A couple of the dreads sustained hull breeches, evidenced by the flames shooting out as the compartment's oxygen burned. As new Sargan ships blinked into the system, they started going after the dreadnaughts three to one.

While those within their quarters of Dread Ten harnessed in their bunks could feel the ship quaking with each volley of the Sargan blasters pounding their shields, they didn't know how desperate the situation had become.

At one point, four battlecruisers fired on them at once. Powering their shields was starting to drain the power for weapons as the battle raged. They shut down all the power to the empty chambers and kept firing at the enemy ships, but some of their weapons arrays weren't firing all the laser cannons.

More of them were failing as the battle wore on; Captain Paulak Ventu was about to call for the personnel in their quarters to arm themselves and prepare for boarding. He had just spoken Dex Jeratu's name to announce the order when four more ships blinked into the battle front. His heart nearly sank.

The shields were failing, and some of their cannons had been knocked out. If more ships started using them for target practice, they just might blow the Dreadnaught apart. Like the Sargans' battlecruisers, a lesser ship would have likely broken apart under such an attack.

The Dreads had taken out a third of the ships attacking them, so the Sargans used the tactic for multiple vessels attacking the dreads one at a time. When the enemy ships blinked into the system, all five of the Dreadnaughts took strategic positions to defend the *Kurellis*.

The Farseek warriors couldn't let the Sargans get close enough to land a boarding party on the passenger ship. If the Sargan's got control, they would take the *Kurellis* and all the people rescued to parts unknown.

Dreadnaught Ten was on point while the

other four maintained a blockade around the massive passenger ship. Captain Ventu blinked and stared at the new arrivals for a few seconds, then breathed a sigh of relief. They were allies, not enemies. Two of them were Consortium battleships, and two were Alliance battleships. With their help, the other four dreadnaughts were able to take control of the battle. The Sargans were soon overwhelmed. Another of their ships was destroyed, and within minutes, the rest of the Sargan's battleships blinked out, leaving at least a dozen fighters behind.

Abandoned by their mothership, the fighters flew off toward the back side of Mecstar Prime. They weren't a priority, so none of the dreads or allies bothered to go after them. They would probably land somewhere on the backside of the planet until the Farseekans and company left and the Sargans returned to retrieve them.

While the battle with the Sargans in space progressed, Narzek was alerted that a shuttle was crashing. He knew what was going on in space, and a slither of fear passed through him for his mate on Dreadnaught Ten. He also knew she would be secured in their cabin, probably the safest spot on the ship.

He couldn't let himself think about it

further, or he couldn't do his job. They were just finishing herding people from the secondary mining site. Narzek had planned to send a couple team members back into the tunnels one more time to check for stragglers.

Instead, he had squad members poll Farseekans to see if anyone was missing while waiting for a shuttle to the *Kurellis*.

Then Narzek's team boarded the borrowed hover tram and headed to the crash site. Pieces of the shuttle were strewn along the landing stretch, still smoldering. It had almost reached the *Kurellis* in space before being forced back into the atmosphere with a damaged engine.

Reentry happened too fast, heating the hull enough to weaken it. The pilot extended the air wings and flaps to slow their descent once they reentered the atmosphere. She used every trick she knew to slow it enough so as not to kill everyone aboard. It still hit the ground too hard, but it broke apart so that the floor in the cargo hold broke loose. It skidded to a stop, only dislodging several of the fifty-some people who had been sitting on the floor.

Narzek started there, dropping off their team field medic and two more team members to help him. They also found more people along the way, still strapped into their seats bolted to the pieces of the floor.

Thankfully, most of the injuries were minor. The worst injuries were among those who had merely been sitting on the cargo hold floor. They'd been thrown off the floor before it skidded to a halt in the dirt. The team medic carried a supply of universal nanocybots, which he injected into the most seriously injured.

Dawn was breaking over the rocky plain where the shuttle crash-landed when they finally accounted for all the passengers from the shuttle. At that point, Narzek got word about the arrival of the Consortium and Alliance Warships. Dreadnaught Ten took massive damage but no fatalities or serious injuries.

Narzek wanted to drop to his knees and thank the Maker for sparing his mate. Instead, he paused for a mini-span and breathed a silent prayer. At that moment, he vowed this would be his last tour of duty into the warzone with Cayla.

He wanted desperately to find his mother, sister, and brother, but he knew he couldn't keep putting his mate at risk to do it. What if continuing the search caused Cayla to be killed, and he still never found the rest of his family? Even if he found them and the process, got her killed, it would destroy him. He was at what Cayla called between a rock and a hard place.

Narzek had to pause for a few deep breaths to clear his mind of those disturbing thoughts. He also had to stop himself from considering the implications of the Alliance ships now orbiting Mecstar Prime with the Dreadnaughts. There were too many variables in the situation to speculate. Meanwhile, he had injured people who needed transport to safety.

He called for a shuttle to come to pick up the passengers from the crash site. Then he went about reassuring them that the fighting was over and another shuttle would take them to the passenger ship safely.

By the time they had gathered everyone together, a second shuttle had arrived. As they left, Narzek sent a voice message to Captain Ventu, recommending the pilot for a commendation. Only her skill kept the damaged shuttle from plummeting to the ground in a fiery explosion that would have killed them all.

Narzek and his team gathered at the hover tram and paused to watch the rescue shuttle take off. They still had kilo-spans before they could return to the ship. The people rescued from that last mining site told them about another smaller site staffed by thirty-four more slaves. At least some of them were Farseekan.

As long as there was a chance to find more of their people, they would keep searching until they were recalled to the ship. Narzek continued to hope that he might find one of his loved ones. Both women and men were forced to work in the mines together.

The crystals mined there were more valuable than what females could earn in brothels. Other than individuals who purchase sex slaves at the auctions, they had more females than they needed for the brothels near spaceports and space stations.

On this tour, they were going to the places with the most significant concentrations of Farseekan abductees. Narzek also considered that his relatives might have been found by any of the other teams.   In that case, he wouldn't know until all the rescues were sorted out on the *Kurellis*.

Mecstar Prime was the last stop for the *Kurellis* before heading back to Farseek. Two of the dreads would be going back with them to the edge of Consortium space, then they would return to rendezvous with the rest of the dreads at their next rescue destination.

Now that Narzek knew his mate was safe,

he could go about the rest of the mission without worrying about her. When he got back, he would make sure she knew beyond a doubt just how much she meant to him.

Chapter Sixteen

Finally, the ship stopped shaking, and Cayla slowly came out of her meditative state. She had no idea how much time had passed or if the attack was over. A minute or two later, the AI voice announced the emergency had passed. All engineering and ship maintenance people were to report for duty, but all the shuttles were still out.

She thought there was nothing for her to do but wait. Then she remembered she could get updates on the rescue operation through the cabin's AI interface. There she learned what had happened.

The extraction of the slaves continued. So far, the only injuries ground side were from the shuttle crash. That meant Narzek was ok. The attack on the ship had halted with the arrival of Consortium and *Alliance* warships.

Cayla's heart stepped up its rhythm as the implications of the Alliance ships dawned on her. It opened a real possibility that she could go... *home*. But, no. She couldn't go anywhere without Narzek.

They were going to Farseek at the end of

this run. She'd learned everything she could about her mate's homeworld. Narzek sent word to the reconstruction board that they would need a home built separately from the main family home. She wasn't willing to give that up, not the new house, Narzek, and the life they planned. They would start a family when they returned to Farseek, and they would farm the land.

Besides, these were Alliance Warships. She doubted they would be taking passengers back to Earth. She did know that there were a few dozen Earthers among the thousands they had rescued already. There were probably more among the Mecstar Prime rescues.

Cayla's thoughts were interrupted when the interface screen beeped with an incoming call from one of the Alliance Warships. She gave the answer command, and an attractive woman appeared on the screen.

"Greetings, Cayla Fox. I am Lieutenant Sherine B'caro. I am the citizen recovery liaison for the United Galactic Alliance of Worlds, which now includes Earth," she said in slightly accented but fluent English.

"Hello," Cayla murmured cautiously, noting that she didn't quite look human. She had blue hair and green feline eyes. She was a Narovian feline. Cayla had met one on the slave ship.

"I understand that you are soul mated to one of the Farseek Warriors. It is my job to assist our Alliance citizens in getting the help they need to contact their families or to secure passage back to their planet of origin if that's what they wish to do."

"I'm not going back," Cayla blurted.

"Understandable," Sherine said. "That is your right. My job is to make sure that you know your options."

"I appreciate that. Our customs are a little different on Earth, but my commitment to Narzek Pardantu is the same as being married to him on Earth."

"That is my understanding, too."

"What I would like is to let my parents know what happened to me. I am sure they think I was killed in the war on Earth. I was reporting for duty when my partner and I were kidnapped by alien slavers. Now I am serving with the Farseek Brigade. We are planning to settle on Farseek when we finish."

"I just need you to answer this question. Have you made this decision not to return to Earth of your own free will?"

"Yes, I have," Cayla said solemnly, meeting the gaze of the female on the screen."

"Thank you, your response has been recorded. Now, if you give me their contact information, I will contact our base on Earth, so they can notify your parents. We will also provide all the com officers information on setting up vid-mail to Earth and other Alliance worlds. Once they set up the system, they will instruct you on how to contact your family."

"Thank you, Lieutenant."

"You're very welcome. If you need any further information, your com officer will know how to contact us."

Cayla nodded both in salute and understanding; then, the screen went dark for milli-span before it resumed with reports about mission progress. They were still evacuating the rescued slaves, with no estimates of when the job would be completed.

Cayla paced back and forth in the small space between the dining table and the sitting area in front of their bedroom nook. She was glad that her parents would finally be notified that she was alive. Now that she had been located, she vaguely wondered what the Army would make of her found status. Technically, it probably made her AWOL, but the last year and a half certainly weren't voluntary.

As far as she knew, Earth didn't even have interplanetary space travel, let alone interstellar capabilities. She couldn't imagine that the Alliance would have any kind of extradition treaty. It wasn't that she didn't want to serve her country; she didn't want to go back to Earth, period.

Besides, no one on Earth would even know she was still alive if the Farseek warriors hadn't rescued her from slavery. She could have been a slave for the rest of her life. Even if the Army decided she owed them for the rest of her enlistment, she doubted they would force the issue. By serving with the Farseek Brigade, Cayla wasn't just serving a country; she was serving Earth.

Undoubtedly, some of the people abducted from Earth and rescued from slavery would want to go back. They still had families and children back on Earth. The Farseek Brigade was freeing them right along with their own people. If not going back to finish her service with the Army made her a fugitive, so be it. From what she heard about the attack on Earth by the Drayids, they were too busy cleaning up that mess to be worried about a couple soldiers abducted by aliens.

Now that the opportunity was real, Cayla wondered if Luanne would choose to go back? Personal communications were restricted as before during the last rescue operation. They were still bringing people up from the planet. Very likely, they hadn't yet contacted Luanne to let her know it was a possibility. But really, they had known that all along. It just seemed more real now that there were Alliance ships minutes away by shuttle.

Cayla paused to read the updates on the com screen. Narzek's team was searching at another of the secondary mine sites. More than a dozen people requested extraction. Shuttles weren't delivering people to the *Kurellis* as quickly. They were touching down in two or more locations for pickups before returning to orbit.

The landing teams were still searching for people to free.

Cayla started pacing again, it could still be hours before they finished, and Narzek returned. She wished that she would be called for duty; she wanted to do more than just wait for Narzek to return.

They had droids for most of the gofer and cleaning work. There were no shuttles to service. Finally, she remembered that she hadn't dictated into her journal that she started soon after Narzek gave her the com tablet. Finally, she stopped and sat down at the dining table.

Instead of the standard entry in Consortium common, she decided to record in

English for her mom and dad.

"Hi Mom, Dad,

I bet you were shocked to know that I am alive and well after all this time. All this time, we thought those people who claimed to be abducted by aliens were making it up. Well, maybe some of them weren't, because that's precisely what happened to Luanne and me. We never even made it to our post.

The next thing we knew, we were on a spaceship, and they told us we were slaves of the Sargus Empire. Luanne and I got separated, but I didn't think we were on the same planet until we were rescued by Farseek Warriors.

They were looking for their people who had been abducted for slavery by the Sargans. I was surprised to learn that Earth is not the only planet in the galaxy inhabited by humans. The Farseek warriors I've met so far are all human, with unique hair, eye, and skin color variations.

This brings me to what I need to tell you; I'm not coming back, at least not any time soon. The Farseek warrior who rescued us has claimed me as his soul mate---they call it solmatu, *and I have accepted. His name is Narzek Pardantu, and I love him very much. We are now mated for life.*

Right now, I've joined the Farseek

Brigade on a mission to rescue the people stolen from his world by the Sargans. One day we plan to go back to his world, Farseek, to settle and start a family.

They tell me that we will be able to exchange video mail for keeping in touch, but it seems unlikely we will come to Earth. It takes months to get there, and we would have to cross a warzone to get to Alliance space.

I love you both very much, and I am so sorry that you probably went most of the time thinking I was dead. I thought of you every day. I worked hard as a slave on a farm, but we weren't abused other than long hours and crappy food.

By the time you get this, you should have the information to respond through the internet.

Love you,
Cayla"

Chapter Seventeen

A full planet rotation passed before Narzek's team returned to the shuttle bay of Dreadnaught Ten. If not for the stimulants and the assistance of his smart armor, Narzek doubted he could lift his weary body from his seat. For the last few spans, it had been hard to keep his mind on the remaining searches. His team members were just as weary, but none of them wanted to leave any slaves on this planet when they left.

He was disappointed that he hadn't found his own family members, but he had seen some from his town that he knew. Narzek still had hope that his relatives could be among the thousands they had evacuated from the planet. It would be at least another rotation before he heard anything.

At this point, his only desire was to fall into his bed with Cayla cuddled in his arms and sleep for half a rotation.

He and his team let their powered armor walk them to the armory, where it retracted from their bodies into their assigned storage module. Narzek pulled on his clothes, stepping into his boots, toeing the switch on each one to fasten them on to his feet. It took an effort of will to set his body into motion and walk the forty yards to the lift to his floor.

The brief respite as it took him up to the third level ended all too soon, and he had to walk another ten yards to his door. He wondered as the door slid open if Cayla would be sleeping.

She wasn't. She was standing in front of their com screen, and she spun around to face Narzek as the door whooshed open. As he stepped inside, the door whooshed closed behind him.

Cayla reached him in three strides, took one look into his tired eyes, and wrapped her arms around him, pressing her cheek against his chest and hugging him. Narzek leaned into her and held her, resting his cheek against the top of her head.

She looked almost as tired as he. Her only rest was during the battle while she was in meditation. All of that happened in about an hour, less than a span, by their measure of time.

Finally, she drew back and tilted her face up to meet his gaze with a tender smile on her lips. Despite his exhaustion, he couldn't resist pressing his lips to hers in a sweet, light kiss.

"Let's get you into bed," she said when the kiss ended. "You look like you're ready to drop, and you're much too heavy for me to pick up."

They shuffled to the bed, and Cayla helped him undress. Then he sat down on the bed while she undressed. When she was naked, she crawled past him to her side of the bed. Narzek lay down beside her and covered them both with the sheet. The last thing he remembered was Cayla's head cuddled against his shoulder and closing his eyes.

Nearly half a rotation later, Narzek found himself in a delightful dream. Cayla was leaning over his naked body on her hands and knees, kissing him and nipping his flesh in little love bites. She had started with his face with just a peck on his lips. She kissed his face all over then moved down to his neck and upper chest.

Her hair was long enough that it caressed his skin as she dragged her mouth over his flesh. He groaned, and his cock went hard even before her lips closed over his male nipple. She sucked and laved one and then the other before continuing her exploration gradually lower on his body with her mouth and hands. It felt so good; he didn't want to open his eyes and lose it.

But when he felt warm flesh brush over his cock, he opened his eyes to see his mate with his cock against her chest between her breasts. She looked up and met his gaze as he watched her and smiled.

"I knew I would eventually get your attention." She smiled at him for a moment and then turned her attention back to his cock. She backed up until her mouth was on the hilt. Sticking out her tongue, Cayla dragged her tongue up the length of it. When she reached the tip, she grippcd it with her hand and lapped her tongue all over the head.

"By the Maker!" he groaned as her mouth closed over the head, and she started sucking on him.

She took it in until it hit the back of her throat, bobbing her head up and down while she worked the rest with her hand, caressing his balls with the other.

He watched in fascination as she brought him steadily toward release. Narzek was about to stop her because he preferred to come in her pussy, but she stopped. Moving up his body on her hands and knees, Cayla poised her opening over his cock head and proceeded to impale herself on it.

Maker, she felt so damn good!

He gripped her waist, helping her as she

moved her channel up and down over his cock. He'd been tempted to roll them over and put her on the bottom so he could pound into her, but watching her ride him was highly arousing. He could feel his orgasm building low in his back, and Cayla was humming and cooing little sounds of pleasure as she neared her orgasm.

Narzek was thrusting up as Cayla descended, panting and sobbing her pleasure until she clamped down on his cock as the first wave of her climax crashed over her. Just a few more thrusts, and he was right there with her, shooting his seed directly into her womb.

Watching her in the throes of her release, Narzek couldn't doubt that she enjoyed sex with him as much as he did with her. It surprised and pleased him that she had been so brazen in taking him.

He wrapped his arms around her and hugged her as she collapsed against his chest, completely spent.

"That was amazing, *me'ara.* Definitely, an enjoyable way to wake up," he said, rubbing her back and stroking her hair. Then he pulsed his cock inside her, causing little aftershocks of her orgasm.

As he held her, his thoughts drifted back to the previous day, remembering the fear that had ripped through him when Sargans attacked the dreads. Even though he knew it wasn't that easy to destroy a Farseek Dreadnaught, there was still a possibility that Cayla could be severely injured. Or killed.

"When this mission is over, I want to resign and go back to Farseek," he said. "The attack by the Sargan's trying to take back the *Kurellis* scared the hell out of me."

"I won't say I wasn't scared, but I believed in the integrity of our Dread. Our cabin was the safest place to be."

"I know, but when I took this mission, it was just me taking the risk. Then I brought you here because we are *solmatu*, and I wanted you with me. You could be going to Farseek instead. Or even back to Earth, now that Alliance ships have arrived."

"Have you heard me complaining? Narze, I was being sent into a warzone back on Earth. You may not think so, but I felt safer on this ship than I felt in that desert. I saw the video of the battle we were in. Dread took damage, but no one was hurt aside from some bumps and bruises."

"What if next time reinforcements don't show in time to even the odds?"

"Then I want every last second I can have with you in the meantime," she asserted.

"Don't even think about sending me anywhere without you."

Narzek framed her face in his hands and met her gaze with a sigh. "I have already thought about it, and I also realize it's not just my decision to make. Mostly, I don't want to be separated from you for however long this mission will take. It could be a star orbit or longer."

He didn't really want to pull out of her moments later, but he had waned. They got up and took turns at the lavatory before sharing the shower and another round of sex before getting cleaned up. By sharing, they only used one allotment of water for that rotation.

A few minutes after they finished their shower and dressed to go to the mess for first meal, Narzek noted their com screen was blinking with a message. He gave the command to play the message. It was from the ship AI.

"Greetings, Lieutenant Commander Pardantu. A member from your list of missing family members, Jakkin Pardantu, has been identified among those liberated from Mecstar Prime and taken to the *Kurellis*. You will receive more information as it becomes available."

Chapter Eighteen

"Jakkin," Narzek murmured, clearly stunned. "Jakkin's alive!" He turned to Cayla, lifting her so they were chest to chest in a fervent hug, turning in a circle. "Oh, Maker of all things! I can hardly believe it."

"I can hardly breathe," Cayla groaned; he was hugging her so tight.

"Sorry, *me'ara*." He loosened his grip but didn't let her down. Instead, he kissed her tenderly, swirling his tongue around hers slowly.

Cayla brought her legs up and crossed her ankles just above his butt, pressing her crotch against his erection. It was an inevitable response whenever her lush body was pressed against him.

Narzek ended the kiss as his stomach growled. It was half a rotation past his last high-energy bar and much longer since his last meal. Still, he was reluctant to release her. He rested his forehead against hers and smiled at her.

"I am so happy for you," she murmured with a light kiss to his lips. "I know you were disappointed when you returned yesterday, but your team found over two hundred people who might have been left behind in those smaller mining sites."

"Yes. But I was glad we found Dias' brother."

"And someone else found yours," Cayla said. "The last report I read estimated that seventy-five percent of the people you rescued were Farseekans."

"That makes me hope that we are on the right path to finding Mother and my sister."

"If they were on the same slave ship, they could have been taken to one of the next star systems on our route."

"We are hoping." Narzek let her down and stepped back, willing his cock into submission. "Most of the repairs on this ship were completed, so we should be moving out of this system soon."

"And the *Kurellis* has already left for Farseek."

"Which means I won't get to com Jakkin. I wish I could have seen him."

"I know, sweetheart," she soothed.

"The news is that the Consortium warships are escorting the *Kurellis* back to Consortium space, so we don't have to send any of the dreads with them," Narzek added, relieved that he was finally presentable as his problem had resolved. "Let's go eat. I'm famished."

"One of the last reports I read before you got back said the Alliance warships were going ahead to the next star system to do recon."

Narzek moved toward the door, and it opened as Cayla followed. They walked to the lift together.

"We found people from Alliance worlds, including Earth, at almost every mine site we explored. That liaison who contacted you also contacted most of them. I think about fifty were transferred to their warships."

"Probably, because Farseek is so far from Earth and Alliance space."

"That was my guess, too. The Alliance has a passenger ship in this sector. They're bound to rendezvous somewhere along the way and much closer than Farseek." They stepped into the elevator as its door slid opened. "We're you even tempted to go when the liaison asked you?"

"Only for a second or two. I just thought about going back to hug my parents one more time," she admitted. "But it passed just as quickly as I thought of leaving you."

Narzek nodded, giving her a slightly rueful look. It was the same reason he could never insist on sending her to safety. In the months they'd been together, she had become a vital part of his life.

Despite the fact their relationship was highly sexual, it was so much more than that. When Narzek and Cayla joined, it was spiritual as well as physical, a celebration of *solmatu*. Sometimes, he was almost positive; he felt her joy at having him inside her.

She had convinced him that she would be as miserable with such a separation as he would. That ended his thoughts about sending her away. If her safety was in question, so was his. She reminded him of that one of the times he brought it up.

It was one of the few times she'd been angry enough that she shouted at him. But it was her eyes full of tears, not her words, that impressed on him what he was asking of her. What good would keeping her safe be if it broke her heart, and his as well?

Narzek could only hope that they both would survive to build the life they planned on Farseek.

Later that rotation, the combined armada of Alliance and Farseek warships left the Mecstar system to pursue a Pican slave ship. This Pican ship was much larger than the average size they usually used. The Alliance had tracked it from their space, and they suspected the Picans carried up to a thousand people abducted from there.

The Alliance wanted those people back, and the Farseek Brigade needed a ship to transport the people they planned to rescue. The Pican ship followed the same course the Farseek Brigade had set for themselves, but they were a couple of systems ahead.

With months until the *Kurellis* delivered their rescues back to Farseek and returned to the Sargus sectors, the dreadnaughts could only collect about five hundred people if they housed them in their cargo holds. Taking the Pican ship shouldn't be too hard for seven warships.

A few rotations later, Commander Lagatu called all the ground teams to a meeting. By then, everyone had received news on whether any of their friends and relatives had been found. Most of them had gotten adverse reports or mixed reports like Narzek. Two of his siblings had been recovered, but one sibling and his mother remained missing.

"First, I want to commend all of you for the tremendous job done seeking and recovering five thousand abductees from slavery. I'm sorry that so many of us were disappointed that our loved ones are still missing. My mate and our daughter weren't found yet, either."

Commander Legatu paced back and forth in front of the podium with his hands clasped behind his back. Then he skirted the stand and took his place behind it.

"I'm not going to soften it for you. So much time has passed that we may *never* find them. I know you don't want to think about that, let alone accept it any more than I do. That doesn't mean we are going to stop this mission.

"We'll keep going and rescuing every enslaved human and humanoid we find. This brings me to our next endeavor.

"As you know, the Alliance ships have been trailing a Pican slave ship that has stolen thousands of their people. We've already rescued some of those they have dropped off on Berrapo and Mecstar Prime.

"We are going to help them seize that ship. An Alliance passenger ships will rendezvous with them once the Pican ship is under our control. We will board and commandeer the slave ship. Then the Alliance passenger ship will dock with the Pican ship and remove the Alliance abductees.

"After that, we will be on our own. Hopefully, this Pican ship will be in better shape than the one we took the last time. We will have about three rotation spans to get it ready."

Commander Legatu paused and let that sink in. "One more thing… The primary reason the Alliance ships saved our asses back there; they were bringing us two hundred Farseekans they rescued. We had about three hundred of their people that we returned to them. Some of our people went with them because they were mated to some of theirs and vice versa.

"A liaison from the Alliance interviewed all of those not returning to their homeworlds to be sure their decisions were completely voluntary," said Legatu. "That's all I have for you today. You will be on light duty for the next three rotation spans, physical training every other span. Dismissed.

As Narzek got up from his chair, he still lamented he hadn't gotten the chance to speak to his brother before he was whisked away on the *Kurellis*. He wondered if Jakkin knew where their mother had been sent. He just wished he'd had the chance to see and talk to Jakkin, period. Realistically, Narzek knew she might be lost to them forever, but he was not ready to stop looking.

He didn't talk to his father about it because Commander Maxin Pardantu chose to remain in a state of denial. His father and mother had been accustomed to long separations all their lives together. They were not *solmatu,* but Yarelle was a member of the Farseek Brigade. They served on the same ship together until she became pregnant and was grounded.

So, Yarelle ran the farm while her mate served in the brigade. Narzek was her firstborn, and they were always close, but he had never been close with his father. None of his siblings were either because he was away so much. Narzek avoided his father as much as possible, which was most of the time since they served on different ships.

Chapter Nineteen

"I just realized that you haven't commed your father once since I've been here," Cayla said. "Does he even know about us?" They were sitting at the table in their cabin, sipping morning tea.

"He was notified of our mating, but I didn't tell him. We don't talk since Farseek was laid to ruin. Truth is, we aren't close," Narzek admitted. "When I was a kid, and he came home on leave, it was clear that he wasn't there to see his children. He was there to rut with his mate, and we were to stay out of his way."

"I'm sorry to hear that. Some people don't make good parents. It's not always their fault. Did you know his parents, your grandparents?"

"Grandfather was killed in the war before I was born. He was a warrior, too. He probably grew up without a father like we did. *Solmatu* was not in the runes for him. I have always sworn that none of my children would grow up feeling the way I felt about him."

"When a kid feels rejected, they either act

out or simply avoid that parent," she said gently and reached across the table to curl her hand around his.

"Mother was a good parent, and our uncle, her brother, used to come and take us on outings. He doted on us, almost like we were his own children. I don't know if he's dead or alive, either."

"At least you have good memories of them. It sounds like you had a strong, caring male role model," she said. "I saw in the reports that the Consortium Warships were liberating slaves as well."

"I haven't given up hope, but I am trying to be realistic and acknowledge the fact that she may never be found. The odds are that I might never see her or my other sister again." He choked up on the last.

Cayla squeezed his hand. "I know, Narze, and I'm sorry."

He closed his eyes and just breathed in and out for a few micro-spans. He wished Commander Legatu had kept his advice to himself. Narzek believed he *had* been realistic about the odds of finding his mother and siblings.

He was a Farseek Warrior, and Farseek Warriors were known to beat long odds against them. The Consortium valued the Brigade and sent its own warriors to Farseek to train with them during the war.

Cayla waited, racking her brain for the right thing to say. Finally, she said, "You have known all along that she might not be found. That doesn't mean you have to accept it as fact. I can't even guess at the odds."

He met her gaze and gave her a sad smile with a slight nod. He took her hand in both of his and brought it to his lips. "Maybe someone found her the way I found you, someone who will appreciate her the way she deserves."

"It just might take a while for her to find a way to let you know she's okay," she said. "Without positive proof that she's not alive, I don't think you have to give up believing she could still be alive."

"Come here," Narzek said, tugging gently on her hand.

She got up, and he swiveled his chair and patted his muscular thigh, smiling up at her. Cayla accepted his nonverbal invitation and sat on his lap, wrapping her arms around his shoulders, hugging him.

"I love you," he murmured, hugging her back.

"And I love you," she said, leaning back to look into his eyes and caressing his cheek with her fingers. She followed that with a light kiss to his lips.

Narzek shoved his fingers into her hair and drew her back to claim her lips in a more thorough kiss, slipping his tongue between her lips to slow dance with his.

In the wake of the despair that led him on this journey, she was the light that shined on his soul. His *solmatu*. Her mere presence helped him keep that despair at bay. She convinced him that he could keep that glimmer of hope, despite what Commander Legatu had said.

Narzek knew putting Cayla on his lap was a bad idea. He went hard almost the moment her lovely ass settled there. Kissing her long and slow only made it worse, but he didn't want to stop. He'd already had her twice that morning, once in the bed and again in the shower. There wasn't time for another round. They were due for training in the gym in a few mini-spans.

Finally, he groaned and reluctantly ended their kiss. "Can you feel what you do to me?"

Cayla giggled and flexed her ass cheeks against his rock-hard cock. "You're hard, and I'm wet, but we don't have time to play." She made a dramatic sigh and got to her feet.

"No, we don't," Narzek said, standing up as well. He picked up his mug and swallowed down the rest of the now tepid tea in his cup as his mate did the same. He concentrated on his breathing and put his mind on the grueling workout ahead of him until his cock settled back down.

After physical training, Cayla went to the shuttle bay to train on a craft also equipped with a simulator. After months of study about everything from maintenance and repair of the shuttles and space flight, she was finally ready for flight simulation.

Cayla was excited to take the next step, even though she knew it could be a long time before she also got to copilot a shuttle. Their mission didn't allow for training flights, mainly because they were in a warzone. However, if she mastered the simulator training, she could go on some rescue runs as an observer and help calm the rescues as they were transported from the planet.

Cayla had been through all the preflight checks numerous times. The constant repetitions were designed to make it second nature and drill them on each test's standard parameters to determine if a craft was flightworthy.

Hykara Elbatu had finally approved her to begin flight simulation. Her supervisor sat in with her as a copilot for the simulation. She simply observed that Cayla went through the procedures. It may have been a simulation, but it was the best Cayla had ever seen. It looked and felt real as she lifted the craft off the flight deck and turned it to exit the shuttle bay.

Lieutenant Elbatu watched her closely and spoke only to acknowledge the flight check as a normal copilot would. In the simulation, Cayla took the shuttle out into space, following a low orbit on the planet until they got close enough to the landing coordinates to begin her descent.

All went well until it came time to return to the shuttle bay. She came in just a little too fast and not quite centered, so she clipped the side of the opening and crashed into another shuttle in the bay.

"Well, at least you didn't kill anybody," Hykara said dryly. "Let's go back and try that again until you get it right. We can't have pilots busting up shuttles, especially when the only way to replace them out here is to steal one."

"Of course, we have enough enemies out here without making more," Cayla quipped.

The next few times she practiced the landing in the bay, Hykara had her just go through the exit and return procedures until she could park that shuttle, just like parking a car in a garage. It took five repeats and most of the rest of the day, but Cayla worked it out.

She was only a little disappointed when Hykara couldn't give her a time frame when she could expect to make an actual flight as a pilot. However, the lieutenant did put her in as an observer for the next planetfall, the next step toward hands-on flight.

She had a feeling it wouldn't please Narzek, and she was right. Cayla could see he wanted to dissuade her from going any further into what could quickly turn into a deadly situation.

"No!" he said. Then he sucked in a breath as he seemed to realize he had said it out loud.

"What did you say?" Cayla demanded, her hands fisted at her sides. She narrowed her eyes, daring him to repeat it.

"No." This time it sounded like a request, not a command. He reached up and pinched the bridge of his nose with his fingers. "I wish you wouldn't. I don't want you to go anywhere; you might get hurt. I've already lost too many people in my life. If I lost you, it would break me. I don't scare easily, but this terrifies me."

"Don't you think I know that? I feel exactly the same when you go out there. Narzek, we're soldiers; this is what we do. I owe these people for what they did to me; the same is you owe them." Her voice got louder until she was shouting at him. She stopped as she realized and took a breath, letting it out in a deep sigh. "In a perfect universe, we would be back on Farseek planting crops and making babies."

Narzek growled his frustration because he knew she was right. She was the love of his life, and she was now a Farseek Warrior, too. But he hated that he didn't have the right to keep her out of this. She wasn't even in his chain of command. Arguing the point was moot.

So instead of taking the argument further, he took two steps closer and hugged her to him, resting his cheek on the top of her head. "I just don't want to lose you."

Cayla couldn't say anything past the lump in her throat. She just hugged him back.

Chapter Twenty

The Farseek Dreadnaughts and the Alliance Raptors arrived in the Ryosan system three rotations later. Two planets and a moon were habitable. The Pican slave ship orbited Ryosa, the largest world. Dreads Five and Six flanked the Pican ship, each sending two squads of warriors to board the ship.

Dreadnaught Ten sent shuttles down to Ryosa with two teams each. That left two teams on standby. Narzek's team was one of the teams making planetfall. He didn't have to worry about Cayla going down on a run because delays at the Mecstar hadn't given them time to send recon before they got into the system. Cayla was set to go on the runs to evacuate the freed slaves. The pickup sites would be secured before she ever left the Dread.

Trouble started before they even landed. The boarding teams faced powerful resistance from Sargan warriors on the Pican ship. Apparently, about a hundred slaves had been replaced by Sargans. As soon as the Farseek warriors relayed their findings back to the dreads, Dread Seven sent another boarding team to assist them. That meant they were only outnumbered three to one. Those were odds they were used to.

As soon as the first teams discovered the Pican slave ship was an ambush, Dread Ten notified the shuttles heading ground side. Before they landed, they did flyover scans for the highest density of humans and humanoids to estimate where they would find the slaves for evacuation. Just as they were getting in range to scan for heat signatures, an alarm sounded, warning them of incoming missiles.

The pilot evaded one, and the computer shot one down, but another hit the shuttle dead on. The shields kept the ship from being blown apart but left the pilot with only marginal control. The shuttle crashed, rolled, and broke apart. The engine section burst into flames and exploded, and the strike teams were strewn over a crop field in full combat armor.

None were moving, and the pilot and copilot were still strapped into their seats in the front section, the only part of the craft that remained intact.

Cayla was in the shuttle bay on Dreadnaught Ten when a com officer reported that Narzek's shuttle had been shot down and believed to have crashed. The shuttle com unit should have been working on battery power even if it was separated from the rest of it. But they weren't getting a signal from the craft or any of the coms in the warriors' armor.

After that announcement, Cayla didn't hear anything else that was said. She even forgot to breathe for several micro-spans until she finally gasped, overwhelmed by the sudden realization that Narzek might not be coming back from this. She could barely face the possibility.

Now she understood his fear more thoroughly than ever before. She stood, staring into space, not seeing anything. She didn't even notice that her instructor and team leader had come to stand in front of her.

"Cayla, I'm taking you off duty, effective immediately," Hykara ordered. "Cayla!"

Cayla met her gaze, nodding vaguely.

"Pull yourself together! The odds are your mate, and the rest of the team survived because they were all in combat armor. They might have crashed in a dead com signal spot. We're sending out two more shuttles with medic droids to search by air for them."

Cayla nodded, "that makes me feel a little better."

"Not good enough for you to remain on

duty. Return to your quarters, and we'll notify you---if--as soon as we locate them."

"Can I go with one of them?"

"I can't let you do that. We're sending a ground unit to search for Narzek's team as soon as we locate the wreckage. You can watch their progress on your com screen in your quarters."

Cayla huffed in frustration.

"I am going to pretend I didn't hear that," Hykara said.

"Yes, ma'am!" Cayla snapped to attention and ducked her head in salute, did an about-face, and strode from the pilot's ready room.

Cayla entered their cabin two minutes later and flopped down in the chair at their dining table, calling out the command to turn on the com screen. She was calmed by the fact that she received a direct feed from both shuttles on the display in a split frame with audio. It was better than the view she would get if she had accompanied them.

Only it didn't allay her fears as to what they might find. She didn't have too much time to fret about Narzek's fate as the entire ship shook so hard it almost threw her from her chair. An alarm sounded almost immediately, with a computer-generated voice announcing they were under attack.

Cayla had already headed for their bunk

to strap in while the order was recited by the AI computer voice in the next sentence. Sighing as she settled into the harness on the bunk, she thought, *maybe we're all going to die today.*

If Narzek was gone, then it really didn't matter. But she didn't really believe he was dead. Cayla was almost sure that she would feel it in her soul if he died while she lived.

The ship quaked again. Cayla squirmed to reach into her pocket for her com. Pushing a hand through a hole in the webbing, she held it so she could see the small screen.

There was a view of space, and several Sargan warships had blinked into the Ryosa system. Apparently, the whole setup was a trap, a concerted effort to take down the Farseek Brigade. So far, they weren't outnumbered because of the two Alliance Raptors in the system with the Farseek Dreadnaughts. The Sargan's main advantage was the fighters that poured from the launch bays of the single battle carrier.

When the Sargan battleships started blinking in near Ryosa, the Farseek and Alliance ships that were strung out through the system moved in. Until they arrived, Dread Ten and Seven were taking a beating from multiple enemy vessels. Soon, all the warships in the star system were engaged in battle, slinging torpedoes and energy beams back and forth.

All were maneuvering to get the best angle with a chance to disable their adversary. Every direct hit to their shields weakened them a bit more, sending vibrations through the whole ship, shaking it hard enough to dislodge Cayla from their bunk had she not been harnessed in. It had made her drop her com a couple times, but it got caught by the harness where she could easily retrieve it.

Cayla knew she didn't really want to die but accepted it could happen. The months she'd had with Narzek were probably the happiest of her adult life. She couldn't let herself believe that's all they would ever have.

She closed her eyes and thought back over their time together, sweet tender moments, shared laughter, the passion of their lovemaking. She couldn't let herself believe that was ending so soon. If she could just hold him one more time…

Narzek's first aware moment, he couldn't understand why his head was pounding with pain. He blinked a few times before opening his eyes and found he was looking up at the sky through the view plate of his helmet. It had darkened to shield his eyes from the blazing sun overhead. He really needed to get up off the ground. He wasn't entirely sure how he had gotten there in the first place.

He flexed his muscles as he prepared to lever himself up. Everything hurt as though he had been body-slammed repeatedly to the ground. Or dropped from the sky.

He groaned. That was it, he realized. They were all dropped from the sky when the shuttle crashed, not just crashed, it was shot down by a missile launched from the ground.

Narzek vaguely remembered giving the order to close their helmets as they were going down. He would be dead had he not been armored for combat. The force of being slammed to the ground could still have caused a concussion and internal injuries.

"Body scan," he ordered from his onboard computer.

"Concussion with extended loss of consciousness, internal hemorrhage from liver and spleen, bruising, nanites injected on impact have stopped blood loss, medications injected to aid healing and reverse concussion. You can now safely ambulate."

Despite what his armor computer told him, it still hurt to move or even breathe too deeply. Probably the crash didn't do his lungs and heart any good either, but the nanites would fix the damage. They always did.

Cayla would probably blanch if he ever told her how many times he had been injured in the war and how badly. Their armor didn't always prevent them from getting hurt but kept them from getting killed most of the time. Then the onboard nanites and meds took away the pain and fixed the damage.

He sat up slowly and requested an analgesic for his pain that would not cloud his brain. It looked like they'd landed in the desert. The ground was rocky with sunburnt vegetation that dried after the rainy season was over. He could see the bodies of his team strewn around like discarded toys and pieces of the shuttle among them.

Chapter Twenty-One

As Narzek stood, he saw the pilot compartment of the shuttle about a hundred yards from where the rest of the shuttle lay. He started pinging their communications channel to see if he could rouse any of the rest of his people while jogging to the intact pilot compartment. He had to pry the door open because there was no power to open it.

Both men were unconscious, but the impact on their bodies had been minimized by airbags deployed when the craft hit the ground with excessive impact. A scan showed they each only had minor injuries.

At that point, Narzek pinged communications on Dread Ten to report.

"LC, we have a shuttle searching for you. I have just sent them your coordinates. All of our ships and the Alliance ships are engaged in battle. We can't safely bring you up right now."

"Understood," Narzek replied, unable to quell a frisson of apprehension that rippled through him.

"Commander Legatu asks if your team

can complete your assignment."

"Affirmative," Narzek replied. "As long as we don't get shot down again."

"Dread Seven Shuttle Two knocked out that rocket launcher, and they will be there to back you up. We need to know ASAP if there are any slaves to evacuate."

"Will do, Pardantu out."

In the time it took the shuttle to arrive, Narzek got his people on their feet and looking for their rifles that were strewn over the ground as they were.

Although he was thinking about it, he didn't say it out loud. How did the Sargan's know to set a trap for them at Ryosa? All of their communications were encrypted, and they hadn't reported their plans to anyone.

During their shuttle trip back to the industrial complex and slave quarters where they were headed before they crashed, Narzek mentally reviewed the list of who could have passed their plan to the Sargans. Someone on any of the ships currently in battle, the Consortium ships, and the *Kurellis* could have found an opportunity to send out a coded message.

He couldn't believe any of those present would have betrayed them. Someone on *Kurellis* was most likely. There were a lot of people they freed that came with little verifiable history. They knew there were Sargan defectors among them, but some of them could have easily lied.

The missile launcher was dead, but a company of Sargans had apparently tracked them and were lying in wait for them at the industrial complex. They weren't much of a challenge for two units of Farseek Warriors with only handheld weapons and substandard armor. The fighting was over in less than a span, and only the Sargans were casualties. They collected those that were still alive and let the med droid attend to them. While the pilots stood guard.

Their original intent was to come in at night and roust their people from the slave residence, a high-rise apartment building that held over a thousand people. Having their shuttle shot down delayed their timetable almost half a rotation.

On the other hand, it didn't really matter because the Sargans worked them in the factories, farms, and mines around the clock. Narzek and the other team leaders conferred and decided the original plan would work and if they started at night. Except, they didn't know if they had transport for the liberated slaves.

Narzek's unit didn't even know if they would get off the planet any time soon. Or if they did, they didn't know who would be coming for them.

There was a weapons factory, a clothing manufacturing plant, and a food processing plant in this complex.

Cayla lay in her bunk for over a span when her com tablet lost the feed of the space battle, and she still didn't know whether Narzek was dead or alive. The ship had stopped shaking, but she wasn't getting any feed at all from the system. Alone in their quarters, her fears overwhelmed her, and her eyes filled with tears. As she blinked, she realized her tears had turned into little globules that floated above her face. Even though she was strapped down, she could feel the loss of gravity.

Now she had, even more to worry about. She mentally shook herself and thought back to her training about what she needed to do in this situation. If the artificial gravity failed, that likely meant the ship had lost power. It could even mean life support had shut down as well. She needed to get into a spacesuit that would keep her warm and provide a few hours of air until she could either evacuate from the ship or engineering restored the power.

Cayla unfastened the harness and held on to it with one hand while she reached for the closet door handle. She opened the metal door and held the handle while taking out the compact suit from inside the helmet. As she opened it up, she was relieved that the helmet was attached to the jumpsuit.

It took a few tries to get it on while wedging the toe of one boot under a foothold at the base of the closet. By the time Cayla got the suit on, her cabin door had slid open, revealing Tagnel Asedtu. He was dressed in an identical outfit.

"Are you all right?" he asked.

"I'm fine." It was mostly true. "What happened?"

"We got them all, but our power grid took a direct hit, and we lost power to most of the ship except for level one. They sent me to get everyone out of the cabins on this level."

"Do you know if they found Narzek and his team?"

"I don't. Maybe some of the others will know."

"Let's see if I remember how to do this." She stretched as far as she could and slid her foot from the hold and lightly pushed off, and reached the handhold by the opening from the bedroom to the tiny sitting area. Then she made it to the doorway and used the handholds to pull herself up to the handrail about two feet below the ceiling.

Cayla continued down the corridor pulling herself along the rail hand over hand to the ladder tube. Tagnel was waiting there with the door open, and he held it for her to go first. It was easy to climb down while she was almost weightless. The lower she went, the more she felt the artificial gravity on level one pulling on her.

Once she reached level one, she could walk to the warriors' ready room, also known as the gym. Cayla and Hykara spotted each other at the same time and hurried over to see her.

"I'm sorry I couldn't get back to you. Narzek's team all survived the crash with minor injuries. Their nanites and medications infused by their armor took care of them.

"Another unit found them and took them to their target."

"Oh, my God!" Cayla sobbed in English, then reverted back to Consortium common. "Thank you, I was going out of my mind."

"They had to fight their way in, but only the Sargans took casualties," Hykara told her. "One of their damn fighters punched through the hull and took out the power relays for half the ship. Engineering is working to rebuild and replace the damaged parts."

Cayla nodded. "Is there anything we can do?"

"All we can do is wait. Dread Eight sent over a couple of their engineers to help. They're estimating three to four spans before it's repaired. Dread Seven sent engineers to the Pican slave ship to fix the air scrubbers in life support.

"The Picans had four hundred slaves still on board. Roughly half of them are from Farseek. They are helping to clean up the cells. The whole place is filthy, except for their quarters. The whole crew has been transported to Ryosa."

"Have they started bringing people up?"

"Yes, and all our ground units are down their rounding them up. They're telling us it will take rotations for us to collect them all, and we don't have room for them all on the Pican ship," said Hykara.

Hykara went on to fill her in on what she'd learned so far about the Ryosa operation. There were thousands of Farseekans and people from all over the Consortium and the Alliance sectors on Ryosa. The Pican slave ship could only take about four thousand, and the accommodations were dismal at best.

Once the Sargan battleships were neutralized, the officers from Farseek ships and the Alliance ships conferred. With almost three hundred thousand humanoids enslaved on Ryosa, the captain decided to call the Consortium and the Alliance for more passenger transports to bring them all home. It could take half a star orbit to locate and extract all the Farseekans, let alone all the other humanoids enslaved there.

There would still be plenty of people to take back to Farseek when the *Kurellis* returned. Meanwhile, the Farseek Brigade needed to revise its rescue plan. Discovering so many of their abducted people on one planet was beyond their wildest dreams.

Chapter Twenty-Two

Narzek spent two more rotations down on Ryosa at the industrial complex while the ground units worked in shifts, sleeping in the shuttles. After securing the compound in their control, they rounded up the overseers to inform them that the Sargus Empire was no more and slavery was outlawed. The Sargus sectors would be split between the Trans-Stellar Consortium and the United Galactic Alliance of Worlds.

If the former overseers wanted to keep their jobs, they had to agree to the terms and code of conduct put forth by the Consortium and Alliance. Next, the slaves were officially freed by a blanket announcement. Those who wanted to return to their homeworlds would be screened in the coming days. They were also informed that the Farseek Warriors had a ship to take Farseekans home.

On the fourth rotation of his assignment on Ryosa, Narzek emerged from the shuttle to begin his shift, and there was a crowd of people waiting to see the Farseek Warriors. Though some of them looked familiar, he only recognized them as Farseekans. He no longer wore his armor now that the complex was secured by Alliance and Consortium soldiers.

Narzek was happy to see so many Farseekans, but he'd almost prefer to be in armed combat than face a couple hundred people looking for answers. In the four days his unit had been ground side, more Consortium forces arrived to secure Ryosa as the world was under their jurisdiction under the treaty with the Alliance. They also sent a massive passenger cruise ship, bigger than the *Kurellis,* to take at least twenty-five thousand Consortium citizens back to their worlds, starting with the industrial complex.

As Narzek explained it to the gathering, a man and woman weaved their way from the back of the crowd. He recognized the male as a Narovian feline. He couldn't see the female with him because she was not as tall. But when they emerged, Narzek was dumbstruck. His eyes teared up, and he stared through the blur as she came forward.

She didn't hesitate to wrap her arms around him and hug him. He hugged her back and finally managed to say one word through the tightness in his throat. "Mom!"

They hugged for a long time, so he didn't see the young woman who came up behind them. When he finally released her, the younger woman came up to hug him, too.

"Pleya!" was all he could say as Narzek hugged his youngest sister.

Everywhere he went, Narzek had hoped he would find them, but he never quite believed he would. When he released his sister, he noted that the feline male had his arm around his mother possessively.

His mother, Yarelle, gave him a faint smile as she noted the question in his expression. "Narzek, I want you to meet Kaver Jensar. He is my *solmatu*, *meomee* in his language. He will be coming back to Farseek with us."

Narzek and Kaver exchanged a polite nod. "I am happy for you, Mother. "What about Dad?"

"We had an arrangement that would end if one of us found *solmatu*. I will notify him as soon as I have contact information."

"I have that," Narzek said. "I also have news. My *solmatu* is in orbit on my assigned Dread. We will be going back to Farseek at the end of my tour." He pulled out his com tablet and showed them a picture of them together.

"She's adorable but so pale," Yarelle said.

"They don't have the skin color mutations

as we do."

"Neither does Narova," said Kaver.

"Excuse me for a moment; I will get someone to cover for me so we can talk for a few mini-spans."

When Narzek returned, he took them off to the side to tell them that Jakkin and Azur were found and would soon reach Farseek together. Although communications were restricted, Narzek got permission to contact his father to let him know Yarelle and Pleya were alive and well and Yarelle to give her news.

Yarelle went off to the side alone for that conversation while Narzek chatted with Kaver and Pleya. They would be getting the new home built on Yarelle's property because that was part of their arrangement.

When Yarelle came back to join them and return Narzek's com-tablet, he could see that she had been crying. "I don't understand why he took it so hard. Even before the attack, I hardly ever heard from him except when he took one of his sporadic leaves to scratch his itch, so to speak." She shook her head and didn't say any more.

Narzek's lips compressed into a thin line. He wondered how they stayed together as long as they had. He suspected they probably enjoyed their physical relationship, but that was not something he would discuss with his mother. He had never seen her look at his father, the way she looked at Kaver.

Too bad for his father. Narzek knew his mother had never looked for another relationship. He would bet her connection with Kaver happened by chance, just like his finding Cayla.

Narzek stayed with them until it was time for him to return to Dread Ten. He wished he had more time with them and that Cayla could meet them before they boarded the passenger ship back to Farseek. He couldn't even com her because all but essential communications were blocked to Dread Ten because of the power outage.

Finally, at the end of his shift, the Farseek warriors were pulling out and returning to their respective ships. Cayla probably didn't even know he was on his way back, so he wasn't disappointed when she wasn't waiting for him at the landing bay. He didn't waste any time returning his armor to the armory and heading to their cabin. It was time for her to be off duty as well.

Cayla had just emerged from the shower and was slipping into her robe when she heard the whoosh of the cabin door opening. She sucked in her breath in a little gasp of excitement. Anyone else but Narzek would have prompted the AI to signal.

"Narzek?" She hurried to the bedroom doorway on bare feet, excited to see him.

He grinned, catching her in his arms in two strides. He lifted her up so they were chest to chest. Cayla wrapped her arms and legs around him and eagerly met his lips with hers. All the anguish of the hours not knowing if he were dead or alive fell away, replaced by the joy of being in his arms again.

They kissed long and slow, savoring their delight in being wrapped in each other's arms.

"I missed you so much!" they murmured together when their lips parted briefly. Then they were kissing again, tongues tangling and making little noises of pleasure.

Cayla was so wet; her naked pussy pressed against his hard cock with his pants between them. She had no doubt where this was going as Narzek shuffled into the bedroom, still kissing her. They fell onto the bed together, with Cayla pressed into the mattress and Narzek on top of her.

"Too many clothes," she murmured, tugging his shirt from the waist of his pants. He raised up so she could pull it up and off.

He pulled open her robe while he toed off his boots, then stood up and dropped his pants. As he paused to enjoy the view of her spread open before him, Cayla looked back at him in all his naked glory and smiled up at him.

She held out her arms, and he bent over her and closed his lips over one taut nipple, sucking it until she let out of moan of pleasure. He moved to the other and did the same to it while reaching down between her legs, dipping into her opening with two fingers while he sucked on her nipple. He rocked his hand back and forth, alternately pressing her clit with his thumb and pushing his fingers into her as deep as they would go.

Cayla cooed and hummed as her muscles tensed with her building climax. She caressed his head and shoulder while he pleasured her until the first wave of her release shook her. She moaned and keened as her body quaked in orgasm.

Narzek leaned over to kiss her mouth as he pulled his fingers out of her. Cayla gave a plaintive little moan. He rose up and shifted her on their bed so she was lengthwise, crawling in after her. She opened her thighs for him to kneel between them, looking up at him expectantly. He lowered himself on top of her and slid his cock into her slick channel, watching her face while she watched his as he filled her.

She saw a reflection of the love and desire she felt in his teal eyes.

Narzek leaned down and pressed his lips first to her forehead, kissing her eyelids, nose, cheeks, and finally settling his lips over hers. She opened for him as the tip of his tongue stroked the seam of her lips. She sighed contentedly as he lowered his chest against her breasts and started pumping in and out of her, slowly at first, then steadily harder and faster.

Soon their hips slammed together in a hard, fast rhythm as they reveled in each other's bodies until their spirits soared to ecstasy and exploded into a starburst of delight.

Chapter Twenty-Three

Sometime later, Narzek commed the mess to send their meal to their quarters. They ate in bed naked, and Narzek told Cayla about everything that happened on Ryosa. He deliberately left out finding his mother and sister until last.

"Oh, Narz, I am so happy for you!"

"She was with a man from Narova, a feline. She said they were *solmatu.*

"What about your father?"

Narzek shrugged. "Father hadn't even visited her in a year before she was abducted. With felines, the attraction is so intense they go into a mating frenzy because of the pheromones the feline exudes when he senses his soul mate."

"Does your father know?"

"I called him so she could tell him. She didn't want him to find out from someone else. I didn't talk to him after she did, but she said he took it hard."

"What did he expect? He neglected her and his family for years. It doesn't sound like she was looking for a new relationship any more than we were. It just happened." Cayla gave him an affectionate smile.

"I also have other news. The Consortium and the Alliance have asked us to stand down."

"Why?"

"They consider our mission a rogue operation. They were on the way to Ryosa when we jumped in ahead of them."

"But we came in with Consortium ships."

"They were coming into rendezvous with the others and get their orders when they arrived. We got here first and jumped right into it," Narzek said. "The High Council has amended its declaration that Farseek is no longer required to provide forces to defend the Consortium. They further declared that the Farseek Brigade is prohibited from doing what we've been doing."

"So, now what?"

"Those who want to continue to shut down the military forces of the Sargus Empire are invited to join the Consortium Defense Force. The Farseek Brigade has been 'invited' to return to Farseek."

Cayla looked at him as though she might not have heard right. "What do you want to do?"

"I want to go back to Farseek and start the life we planned when this was over," he said.

"It's over for me---not just because I found my family. I've spent ten years of my life fighting the war with the Sargan's only to have them attack our homeworld before the peace treaty was ratified."

Narzek set his food plate on the auto cart, took Cayla's from her, and then pulled her onto his lap. She cuddled against him and put her head on his shoulder. "When I knew we were going to crash, the last thing I remember was thinking if I died then, I would never hold you again, or couple with you or watch you grow round with our child in your belly. I could have died before I even found my mother and sister."

He paused to give her a tender kiss. "What do you think?"

"I think I love you with all my heart, and I want what you want."

"I love you, too, and this Dread is taking us home."

Then there were no more words as Narzek proceeded to love her with his body as well as his soul.

It was about a month and ten days or a quad span into their journey to Farseek when Cayla received a return vid-mail from her parents Jean and Ken Fox. Cayla choked back a sob as they came on the com screen in their cabin, sitting on the familiar sofa in their living room.

"Cayla, sweetheart, we were so happy to hear your voice and see your face. When the Army came and told us you were missing in action, we were sure you were dead," said Jean. "We probably wouldn't have believed what actually happened if the Alliance hadn't announced their presence on every TV and radio in the country."

"They sent agents to tell us how you had been abducted and sold into slavery," said Ken. "We are so glad those soldiers rescued you and your friend Luanne. ...And now you married one. I—We wish you were coming home to us, but knowing that you are alive and happy with a man who loves you... That was the best news we could have gotten."

"Things haven't been the same since the Drayids attacked Earth. The Alliance stopped them and sent them back to where they came from, but so many people lost loved ones in the cities that were attacked. We were just lucky not to live near any of them. But people are not the same... Now that we know there are beings out there with the power to destroy our world as if we haven't been doing it fast enough ourselves," said Jean. "That was a

while ago, just after we learned you were missing."

"They said you were going to a place called Farseek, a world like Earth was before overpopulation and pollution. We can't wait for you to send pictures," said Ken. "And we want to see pictures of this man Narzek who has claimed your heart.

"There's not much more we can tell you. We love you and miss you, and we can hardly wait to hear from you again."

By then, Cayla was sobbing, and Narzek got up from his seat at their table and pulled her up into his arms. He took her to his chair, putting her on his lap, holding her as she cried on his shoulder.

He almost felt guilty for taking her even further from her home. Almost. Some day when the combined forces of the Alliance and the Consortium got control of the Sargus territories, maybe they could visit Earth. But there was no guarantee, so he didn't suggest it.

He would just have to love her enough for both of them. That, he could do.

Epilogue

A year and a half later (a star span) on Farseek

"What a great day for this!" Narzek said, watching the women chatting together and sipping ale from a glass with his friends.

He and his warrior friends had gathered with their families at his family home to celebrate Freedom Day. While it wasn't the exact day that the Farseek Brigade arrived on Ryosa, it was just the date they chose to commemorate it. Ryosa was only one of the many worlds abducted Farseekans were taken. Just over four hundred thousand had been returned or at least freed from slavery. Some had made new lives for themselves elsewhere.

Since returning to Farseek, Cayla had become friends with Kragyn's mate Reanne and Argen's mate Zoey. Both Reanne and Zoey were visibly pregnant, and Cayla just learned she was pregnant too.

Cayla's friend Luanne was not pregnant yet, but they all figured it was only a matter of time. Luanne had found her soul mate in a

Narovian feline on the *Kurellis,* who was on his way to Farseek to start a new life. They were *meomee;* fate made a choice for them.

Cayla had learned to fly shuttles transporting goods and passengers from spaceships orbiting Farseek. Argen Trematu started his own company and hired Cayla and a couple other pilots from the Farseek Brigade. She worked a few rotations per span. The rest of the time, she helped Narzek on their farm.

It was the life they planned when they weren't sure they would make it back to live it.

But they all did, and they were happy. This day was all about celebrating life and freedom.

THE END

Clarissa Lake's other works:

Narovian Mates Series
Dream Alien
Alien Alliances
Her Alien Captain
Her Alien Trader

Farseek Mercenary Series
Commander's Mate
Lieutenant's Mate
Sahvin's Mate
Argen's Mate
Faigon's Mate

Farseek Warrior Series
Kragyn

Wicked Ways

Interstellar Matchmaking
Korjh's Bride
Rader's Bride
Joven's Bride

Cyborg Awakenings
with Christine Myers
Jolt Somber
Talia's Cyborg
Axel Rex
Dagger Jack

Cyborg Rangers
Blaze

Szeqart Prison Planet Series
Soliv Four
Coraz

15214838R00119